VOICES IN THE DARKNESS

Talia's mother: "All you have to do is *eat* and everything would be all right."

Talia's father: "Something wrong with Talia? Nonsense. Talia's always been *perfect*."

Talia's husband: "Do you realize how long it's been since we had sex? *Seven months*."

Talia's psychiatrist: "You do have to go to the hospital. *Otherwise you'll die*."

Talia herself: "They don't know it but I'm better than they, stronger than they—*if I don't let them weaken me with food*."

ALABASTER CHAMBERS

"Excellent and realistic!"—*Atlanta Journal*
"Sensitive and straightforward."
—*Kirkus Reviews*

Big Bestsellers from SIGNET

ALABASTER CHAMBERS

EMILY ELLISON HUDLOW

A SIGNET BOOK

NEW AMERICAN LIBRARY

TIMES MIRROR

NAL BOOKS ARE AVAILABLE AT QUANTITY DISCOUNTS
WHEN USED TO PROMOTE PRODUCTS OR SERVICES. FOR
INFORMATION PLEASE WRITE TO PREMIUM MARKETING DIVISION,
THE NEW AMERICAN LIBRARY, INC., 1633 BROADWAY,
NEW YORK, NEW YORK 10019.

This is an authorized reprint of a hardcover edition
published by St. Martin's Press, Inc.

SIGNET TRADEMARK REG. U.S. PAT. OFF. AND FOREIGN COUNTRIES
REGISTERED TRADEMARK—MARCA REGISTRADA
HECHO EN CHICAGO, U.S.A.

SIGNET, SIGNET CLASSICS, MENTOR, PLUME, MERIDIAN, AND NAL
BOOKS are published by The New American Library, Inc.,
1633 Broadway, New York, New York 10019

First Signet Printing, July, 1980

1 2 3 4 5 6 7 8 9

PRINTED IN THE UNITED STATES OF AMERICA

To
My Parents
With love and respect

=== 1 ===

Talia had watched her all evening. She had disliked her intensely, this woman whose arms rippled and swung loosely; unexercised, over-pampered, floured folds of arms that stirred the air when she talked, taking up more room than her conversation warranted.

The bulk of the woman was obscene, her massiveness making even Rubens's Baroque women appear lean in comparison. Her buttocks, Talia knew, must be like so many sides of beef, dimpled and depressed as if pounded periodically by a mallet, and her inner thighs chafed and raw from having been kneaded by one another when she walked. Her breasts were two shrinking oranges which had remained uneaten too long; the pulp had gone sour and the peel had shriveled and was covered with a fine, green dust of growth. Talia wanted to brush it away; it was only Jovan or Chanel, of course, but it irritated her nonetheless as it settled in the tiny furrows of the soft, flabby skin.

Talia's mother would detest this woman; Talia was fairly certain of that: this uncontrolled woman expanding over half the length of her sofa, the sofa Mother had helped her choose. No; not helped choose, actually; chosen. But, as always, Mother had not been incorrect. The lines of the furniture were pleasing, the nap held well, and the color was both attractive and durable. And Michael had liked it—it was expensive. *Too* expensive. Talia had agonized for weeks over the cost, and now this woman was soiling Mother's selection with decomposing ooze. Each time she leaned forward to select a canapé, Talia was certain a stain

1

would remain where the heavy arm had been sprawled and the bosom-fruit would roll to the floor as if falling from a busted crate.

The withered oranges were exposed now, slightly, as the guest bent forward to sink a spear of raw broccoli into avocado dip. Talia could see the bland condiment had separated; liquid floated on top, and avocado was dried and caked around the container's rim. Such a waste!—the food should have been refrigerated hours before, not left out so long after dinner. Michael had told Talia she would need assistance with this party. He kept telling her she should hire someone to help serve and clean up afterward. But it had seemed so unnecessary an expenditure. Mother always managed alone; Talia should be capable of doing the same. Still, perhaps she should have sought help. Michael was always correct; he and Mother.

A hand touched Talia's shoulder. The malleable, boneless hand of a man Talia was supposed to know. Chairman of the board, was that what Michael had said? "Be especially attentive to this man, Talia," Michael had said. "Listen to everything he says."

"Michael tells me you've returned to school. Studying business, are you?"

"No, sir."

"We're putting lots of women in management these days." He crammed a melting *petit four* into his mouth, his words falling heavily upon Talia like dollops of leavened dough. "There is no place like the airlines, Talia, for women to get ahead." He licked icing from his fingers in a manner both grotesque and greedy, then watched Talia, expecting, as everyone always did, something from her.

"No, sir, I'm not," Talia said. "I mean, I'm not studying business. Literature. I'm working on my master's in English Literature."

"Ah, yes. Literature. Commendable."

Peripherally, Talia could see that Michael was watching her, moving her way, checking on her. She must talk with this man, must show Michael she was able to handle the situation.

"May I get you another drink?" she offered.

"The little wife is ready to go. Can't stay out late like we once did," he said, winking at Talia like a fool, then turning to help his wife to her feet. He was married to the pudgy lady on the sofa. It was obvious: the same pudding features, pasty skin, tumescent sacks under each eye. But somehow he carried it off better than she; tweed seemed to cover it better than plunging mint lace. And then, too, it was always easier being a man.

"It was a lovely party, dear," he was saying to Talia now. "Excellent food," and he touched her again with one of his enormous, soggy hands. She so disliked this sort of thing: amenities, social discourse. And she despised his touching her this way. She wanted him to leave, to take his little (!) wife home before she ruined Mother's sofa.

"You and Michael must come for dinner after the holidays," the woman said, rising, miraculously leaving no stain. "Just the four of us."

"My Eda's quite a gourmet," the man winked again and his wife grinned fatuously, exposing tainted teeth.

"She likes to cook?" Talia said.

But there was no answer as Michael joined them, taking the woman's hand. "You and Eda aren't leaving, are you, Cleve?"

Talia had known Michael would come; interfere. All evening he had followed her about, listening each time she was forced into conversation, fearful, as Mother always was, she would say or do something wrong. He had insisted that they have this party (knowing Talia's aversion to such things) and had drilled her continuously concerning the guests; told her exactly what she should say, every comment carefully weighed, each statement meant to please and impress. "For the sake of business, Talia," Michael had explained. And for the sake of business these people—wealthy, influential people; people Talia distrusted, disliked—had been invited to her home. Michael, of course, was in his element with people such as these. He knew how to handle himself, said the correct things. It was one of the things about Michael she most liked—his openness, his easiness with people. If only she weren't expected to be partner to his ways; if only she could stand back, invisible, and watch.

"Say good night to our guests, Talia." He glared at her now, although his voice was amicable, as he placed a mink around the woman's shoulders. Talia wanted so to laugh at his gesture, this caricature of Michael dressing a pig. But Michael wouldn't like that thought, not about this man's wife. And from the way he stared at Talia now, she felt he had picked up the current of her thinking. Sometimes she believed he could do that, knew what she was about to say even when the thought wasn't truly solidified in her own mind.

"We had a lovely time, dear." The woman's pouch of a chin kept time with her jaw as she spoke to Talia. "You must give me the recipe for the artichokes."

"Yes, I will." Talia said, turning her cheek as her guest planted a kiss and gave her a formidable hug, knowing she would do no such thing. The recipe was hers, given to her by Mother, and not to be shared. As she pulled away from the woman, smelling the slightest whiff of citrus (she was almost positive of the scent), she looked quickly at her clothes, fearing they might have been marked by the woman's powder of mold.

Talia stood inside the open door now, waiting, as Michael walked the couple to their car. There were still ten or twelve people in the living room, and Talia knew she should go to them, "mingle," as Michael would say. But instead she waited for him, parrying future conversation as long as possible.

"Get inside, Talia, it's freezing out here." He came running back up the walk, breath visible as he talked. It was two days before Thanksgiving and Atlanta had already hit an autumnal low colder than all of last year. There had been a time when Talia would have permitted herself to acknowledge the low temperature, to be cold-natured, sleeping with three or four blankets in the winter, never going out without being properly wrapped. No more; she didn't allow it. She felt no sensation now of either heat or cold. "Get inside, Talia! You're like ice."

By the time she had the door closed, Michael was with another group of guests huddled near the fire. Someone had him cornered now, asking of business, discussing the hijacking profile he had worked on for months. "You and your psychiatrist friend get that report finished up?" Talia heard someone ask and watched Michael being drawn further into the circle of his associates, eager to discuss his job.

That was good, Talia thought; with his mind on other matters he wouldn't be following her; she could slide back into the kitchen with the hors d'oeuvre trays and he would never notice. She bent to pick up a half-empty silver tray, knowing she must remove the food from the living room before she was driven insane, and as she did so, a hand touched hers.

"Janus, I didn't see you. Would you care for more? A drink?" Talia said.

"Relax, precious. You've been rushing around all evening. Enjoy yourself."

Talia positioned herself upon the sofa and secured her body against its arm. This perfectly dressed and manicured woman, with her divinity-like face and too-sweet expressions, had eyes that locked Talia in place and left her unable to move. Her throat felt as if she were swallowing cotton, making it impossible to speak, and her hands shook so badly she hid them at her sides. Janus, in comparison, was as elegant and cool as asparagus, her body a slim, tight rod of perfection.

Last spring Talia and Michael had spent a weekend with Janus and her husband, Paul, at their second home on Sea Island off the coast of Georgia. Each morning Janus would descend the stairs, her milk-white powder pressed evenly over her face, her lips outlined and glossed, her hairstyle as perfected as that of a model. Michael had been blatantly impressed, but more by Janus's money, Talia thought, than by her impeccably maintained and faultless body. But Talia had found their wealth disconcerting, wasteful even, from the moment she and Michael had driven onto their shelled drive and had seen the multi-tiered, pink, wedding-cake stucco which was their home. Since that visit, Talia had thought of Janus and Paul in terms of that house, seeing them as the bogus bride and groom on top: plastic dolls positioned on an enormous slice of pretension.

Janus was scrutinizing now: "You've lost weight, haven't you?"

"A little; yes, thanks."

"Paul and I want you and Michael to go skiing with us this winter." Janus lit a cigarette with a lipstick-red lighter and blew the smoke toward Talia. "We go to a place my parents own near Vail. Michael would love it if you could pull yourself away from your studies for a while."

"I don't ski."

"You're an intelligent girl, honey. You could learn." Janus made tiny revolutions with her wrist, letting ice circle around the walls of her glass.

"May I get you another of those?" Talia said, staring at the drink. The clinking of ice gnawed at her nerves.

"I'm only waiting for Paul. If I can find the darling, I'm ready to go."

"I saw him in the den," Talia said, realizing she said it too quickly, too eagerly. And then, because Mother had taught her extremely good Southern manners: "Are you sure I can't get you another drink?" all the while wanting the woman to leave.

"Positive." Janus blew the last puff of smoke over Talia's head and put the butt out in an Imari ashtray Talia held before her. "Keep in mind the trip to Vail. And," she tossed over her shoulder, "take care of yourself, dear. You don't look well."

Other guests were beginning to gather near the front of the house now, preparing to leave. Talia ran to a closet in the foyer, pulling out jackets and coats, wanting to hurry them all.

"Beautiful! Exactly who I was looking for, the hat-check girl." Talia cringed at the sight of Frank Stoner. She did not know whether it was because Mother would think this man a churl or because Michael so detested him that she found Frank impossible to stomach.

"Is this yours?" Talia held up a leather coat, hoping it was Frank's so that he might go.

"You betcha, doll. Who else could afford a coat like that?" He flicked his cigarette absently, and Talia stiffened as she watched the ashes fall. "Come here, Tally babe, and give old Frank a hug." He drew her face toward his with a damp hand on the back of her neck. "It's been a ball. Absolutely. You were your usual vivacious self." The amalgamating smells of liquor and tobacco on Frank's breath caused the lining of her abdomen to rise in a tight metallic mass and lodge in the center of her throat, her mouth tasting of lead.

"Leaving, Frank?" Michael said, taking the coat from Talia, extending it to his guest.

"I was telling your charming wife here what a pleasure it's been. Wouldn't have missed it for the world. A blast." The cigarette hung in his mouth as he pulled the coat on over his arms. As Talia turned for an ashtray, burned tobacco fell against Frank's shirt.

"Damn it!" He smashed the butt into the container Talia now held out to him. "Nasty habit. But my only!" he said, pointing one finger in Michael's direction. "Mustn't forget that, Michael boy," then he pulled Talia to him again, slobbering upon her neck as she held her breath, hoping not to drown in the crassness of this man.

Together, Talia and Michael stood on the front steps of their home, his arm around her waist as the remaining guests warmed up their cars and began backing out the drive. Michael was a master at creating this kind of scene, this Rockwellish guise: loving couple in front of their home; Thanksgiving wreath on the door; smoke from the chimney; arms raised in friendly good-bye. It was ludicrous! Talia thought, and wanting no part of it, pulled away from Michael's hold and started to turn.

"I'm going in," she said.

"Not yet, you're not." He tightened his grip around Talia's waist and held her against him until the last automobile was at the bottom of the drive. As the car pulled into the street he gave one final wave and bent to kiss Talia's cheek. Scene complete.

Michael's arm dropped like an anchor and he steered Talia through the threshold. With one hand he slammed the door and slapped at the front light switch with the other.

"You really enjoyed yourself, didn't you?" he said.

"Must you shout?"

"Everything's a shout to you. God, it's like living in a convent." He picked up one of four crystal decanters on the bar and poured. "We almost ran out of this stuff. I told you we'd need more." He stirred his drink and then walked toward Talia, the swizzle pointed at her face. "I told you to order more."

"We got by," she said and began stacking glasses on a malachite tray.

"Talia, this party was important to me. Don't you understand? Honey, look," he took her hand. "I need a little help from you right now with these business things."

She pulled away. "You're making an issue over a bottle of Scotch."

"Damn it, Talia! The issue is the impression we make," he said, spilling his drink as he slammed it to the table. "These people are important. My career is at stake. Goddamn it, Talia, put down that tray and listen to me."

With slow and deliberate movements Talia placed the green salver on the mantel and faced him, a hand cupped behind her ear.

"Hell, it isn't worth the effort." He wiped his hand across the bottom of the glass, flinging spilled liquor to the floor. "We ran out of ice three times." He waited. "I *said*, we ran out of ice."

"I heard you."

"I think you planned it. The whole thing was a ploy."

She ignored him, trying to muffle his shouts with thoughts directed at her task of clearing the tables of drinks and ashtrays.

"You wanted to mess this party up, didn't you?" He poured himself another drink, stirring it with his index finger. He licked the finger and again jabbed it her way. "You'd better not blow this thing for me, Talia."

"Do you really need that drink?"

"Hell, yes, I need it. Look at yourself, Talia. You look sick!"

"Don't start that again."

"And that dress. Why the hell did you wear it? I told you what to wear. Picked out the shoes and everything. The matter was settled. Next thing I know you're walking around in that sack. That ridiculous rope tied around your middle. Why the hell did you change?"

"I wanted sleeves."

"I thought you said you're never cold anymore."

"Would you like coffee?"

"I still can't believe you wore that thing. It was humiliating. I told you what to wear."

"I changed my mind."

"You ran around here, picking up glasses, sticking ashtrays under everyone's nose."

"I don't like a mess."

"You're a perfect maid."

"Go to bed, Michael."

He followed her into the dining room and through the swinging door to the kitchen.

"But the biggest embarrassment of all was dinner."

"My food was good."

"Sure. On the first serving. But you kept shoveling garbage on their plates until it was running on the floor."

"It wasn't garbage." It wasn't! She'd worked for days perfecting the menu.

"How would you know? You never touched the stuff."

"You're inebriated," Talia said.

"Not nearly so much as I'd like. I couldn't believe you didn't eat."

"Go away. You smell of alcohol."

"Why didn't you eat?"

"I ate."

"The hell you did! Put down those dishes and look at me. I want to know why you didn't eat a goddamn thing all fucking night."

"I *wasn't hungry*."

"What does hunger have to do with it? It's a social thing."

"I really don't care."

"You'd better care. You'd better start caring about a great deal of things, Talia."

"Go to bed, Michael."

"I'm tired of your stupid diet." He was shouting again, each word a painful blast within Talia's sensitive ears. "It's gone on long enough. You haven't eaten in days."

"I told you, I was not hungry."

"You know what you look like?"

"I look fine."

"You look old, Talia."

"Go to bed, Michael."

"Not until you eat. Not until you put something in that twisted little mouth."

"You're being obnoxious. Leave me alone." Talia turned away.

"I told you. I'm not going to bed until I see you eat."

"I'm not a child."

"You're acting like a child—I'll treat you like one. Now sit down." He slammed a dinner plate on the table.

"You're going to break something."

"I told you to sit down."

"I'm not hungry."

"I said, sit down." Michael went to the silver drawer. "Believe me, Talia, you will sit down," he said and threw a spoon at the plate. Pulling her by the wrist, he led her to a chair."

"You're hurting me."

"Now eat!" He pushed her up to the table by the back of the chair.

"Michael, stop it. *Please.*"

"Here, try the veal. Isn't that what you insisted everyone try?"

"Stop it!"

"And the soufflé?"

"You're going too far—"

"Spinach? By all means; you'll definitely want the spinach."

"You're ruining it, Michael."

"Now pick up that spoon."

"No."

"I said, pick up that spoon."

"I can't."

"Okay, I'll do it for you." He filled the utensil with vegetables and pushed it toward her.

"Michael, *please.*"

"Open your mouth."

"No, you won't do this." She snatched the spoon from his fist. Bending her head and covering her face with her left hand to prevent Michael from being able to see, she took a bite. "There. I've eaten."

"Not enough."

"I'm full."

He pushed the plate closer.

"Michael, I can't do this."

Grabbing her wrist, he forced the spoon back in her hand. "You will eat, or I swear I'll force it down your throat."

Yanking the plate off the table and holding it close to her chest, Talia turned in her chair, her back to Michael.

"What are you doing?" he said and pulled at her shoulder.

"Eating. Leave me alone."

"I can't see you."

"Leave me alone!" She jerked free of his grip.

"You're to eat it all. Every bite."

Talia grabbed the last of it and turned around, throwing the empty plate across the table, the spoon still in her hand.

"Wasn't so difficult, was it?"

"Get out of here!"

He pushed away from the table. "I don't suppose you're coming up?"

She held the spoon in both hands, wanting to bend it in half.

"Okay, sit down here and sulk awhile," he said. "That'll do you good. Lock the doors when you come up and turn out the lights."

"And brush my teeth?"

"What?"

"I said good night."

Talia locked the bathroom door.

Damn Michael! He couldn't do this. It was hers: her only thing.

She looked at the image before her in the huge mirror over the sink. What had he said? She looked old? No. He was wrong. Michael was trying to ruin it.

She untied the sash from her waist and pulled the dress over her head. God! all that food. It pushed at her ribs. She was so full. She pressed against her stomach with the fingertips of both hands; the bulging abdomen pushed back.

Michael was a fool. He should be proud, but instead he chastised her. Michael was jealous; that was it. Jealous because he was not as strong as she. But now he had taken that away too. He had forced her to eat. How could she be so weak, submit to such vulgar demands? She looked again at her reflection in the glass, at the repulsive accretion that was her stomach. She must correct this! She *must*.

Carefully, she folded a towel and placed it on the floor beside the commode. She knelt. The sound— Michael mustn't hear. She quickly stood again and turned both handles at the sink. The water rushed full force. Now the shower.

She knelt again, straightening the towel, smoothing and circling it around the curve of the commode. "You will not do this, Michael," she said aloud, the words obliterated by the drumming of water. He could not usurp what was hers.

Rising on her knees, she held her hands together in front of the bowl. It was the illustration Arthur Rackham had painted of Pandora and Epimetheus kneeling nude before the box. And Talia would be filling the box, of course, rather than letting evils out. She would purify herself.

Steam was filling the room now; it would cleanse her poisoned pores. Bending over the toilet, Talia saw herself reflected in the water below. She stuck a finger down her throat and heaved. Again! Her fingernail stabbed her palate. Nothing. She wiped watering eyes and blew her nose. She tried again, her hair touching the seat. With two fingers she jabbed her epiglottis, gagging. Body rebelling, she vomited on the contorted image below.

2

Edible patterns flowed over the plate. Tesserae of eggs, grain, and butter formed Talia's mosaic.

"Feeling better this morning?" Michael said.

Talia ignored him as he rinsed his eyeglasses—a parody of tortoiseshell, heavy and as broad as his jaw—under a stream at the kitchen sink. He was the slightest bit nearsighted, needing the glasses only at the theater or when he drove. But he wore them continuously, claiming, "It adds to my credibility, more mature, don't you see?"

Michael moved from the sink now and placed a hand at Talia's back. "Honey, about last night . . ." he said and rubbed the hand along her spine; as he did so she recoiled, the touch sending a message to her brain that prickled her neck and scalp. The hand stopped, and Michael stood behind her for a moment before he spoke, his words aimed at her this time like shards of steel: "Up all night, weren't you?" he said.

Talia arranged parsley, adding new texture to her design.

"Talia, I'm talking to you."

"Yes, I was up."

"What were you doing?" He dried the lenses with a paper towel and then held them to the light. "Talia, I asked what you were doing all night."

"Studying."

"Well, you're getting circles under your eyes. It looks bad."

"I can't sleep."

"So you tell me." He sat at the place she had set for

14

him at the kitchen table, the steaming mosaic before him.

"Those are cheese grits," Talia said, "and the muffins are hot."

"I don't know why you go berserk in the mornings. Some coffee or juice would do. And possibly a comb through your hair." He wrapped a large, square hand around a mug.

"That's a new recipe on the muffins."

"Must you wear that robe, Talia? The thing looks like you've had it since you were ten."

"The buttermilk causes the lumps."

"I love this conversation. Talia, I really don't need a breakfast like this. Did you hear me?"

She pushed a basket of warm bread toward him. "A breakfast is fundamental in getting started."

"That applies only to me, I suppose. You're a paradox, my dear."

"There's more coffee. I made a pot."

He nodded absently, giving Talia his cup. "Who was that on the phone?" he said.

"Don't let your eggs get cold."

"Talia, the telephone. Who called? I heard it ring as I stepped into the shower."

"My mother," she confessed.

"What'd she want this time?"

"We're having lunch."

"Today?" He wiped a napkin across tight lips. "What about school? I thought you had an exam."

"Michael, you didn't finish."

"Talia, what about school?"

"There are more muffins. You have to eat one more." Talia buttered one of the warm cakes and extended it toward him.

"She still runs things, doesn't she?"

"They're so much better when they're warm. Try it, Michael, please?"

"When are you going to cut the cord, Talia? Or do you plan to keep running every time she picks up the phone?"

"She's driving all the way from Athens to see an art show at the High Museum. The least I can do is have lunch with her when she's in town."

"I don't get it. You stay up night after night to study, and yet all she has to do is call and you sacrifice everything, even school, for your mother." His eyes were tarragon: the color growing stronger as he angered.

"She's my mother, Michael. Where are you going?"

"To work."

"You didn't eat your eggs, Michael!"

"Go meet your mother, Talia. I'll see you tonight."

Talia had labored on the breakfast since six—found the recipes during the hours of the morning when she couldn't keep her mind on her studies and couldn't sleep—and Michael hadn't eaten his eggs and had barely touched the grits. He was cruel and wasteful, Talia thought, as she folded the abandoned food and carefully eased it down the sink's throat.

Mother's lack of punctuality was a glaring imperfection.

She and Talia were to have met at twelve. It was eight after as Talia stood near the escalator on the second floor of Phipps Plaza; waiting. She glanced at her watch again; nine minutes now, wasted and lost forever.

Talia thought of waiting in the bookstore across from the restaurant, but then thought better of it, fearing she and Mother might miss in the crowd. Instead, she peered through the smoked windows of the store at row after row of precious volumes, carefully bound and shelved. There was a time when the sight of books would have drawn Talia as a dog to the smell of food. She would wrap herself in them, hide between their pages, and devour their words. But lately books, like her studies, were unable to satisfy her as before.

A line had formed outside the restaurant now and

curved toward Lord & Taylor, the waiting procession sliced into small sections of twos, threes, and fours. A giggling pair of buxom girls chewed on bagels as they waited in line. The more corpulent of the two spread white cheese evenly over her roll with a thick stub of a finger and then jammed the last of it into her mouth. Talia counted the chews; only six. The girl was a fool—she made the journey twice as difficult, caused the muscles of her stomach to work twice as hard to propel her food the entire thirty feet. If the girl was so stupid, she deserved to be rotund!

"Talia." The word splashed like Chablis against glass as a finger tapped Talia's shoulder. She had sensed Mother before the address or the touch. The smell of Joy had permeated Talia's world since she was a child. She could catch the slightest suggestion of the fragrance in a crowd and immediately suffer a filial pang, perceiving the scent as Mother.

"You're fifteen minutes late," Talia said, accepting an embrace. Mother pecked Talia's cheek, then rubbed at the red smudge with a laced handkerchief; each action irritatingly familiar to Talia.

"Then you're ready, I presume."

"Mother, we were supposed to meet at twelve."

"You sound like Daddy."

"Must you call him that?" Talia said.

"Look at the line. You didn't make reservations, of course?" She looked at Talia for confirmation. "Fortunately I did. I was standing in front of that painting of Seurat's, "Afternoon in the Park," when I thought of a crowd."

"You have the wrong name."

"I'm certain it was Seurat."

"The painting. It's not a park, it's an island."

"Island, park, whatever; let's get you fed. You're starving, I know. You don't look well," Mother quickly surveyed, then walked past Talia, erect and proud, with that long, fluid stride. She was three inches taller than Talia, but the distance had always seemed much more. She appeared lofty, her head elevated high above her Nefertiti-like neck; her angular shoulders seemingly designed for flight.

"Sinclaire. Reservations for two." Mother enunciated clearly, her words pouring forth with an accent characteristic of Athens, Savannah, and old Mobile.

They followed a short, squat young man through the restaurant to a table for four; Mother first, towering like a caryatid above him, and Talia, insignificant, trailing behind.

"Would you care for cocktails?" the man asked, turning to Mother, then Talia, his smile too seasoned to be real.

"We're here for lunch. A menu, please," Mother said and pulled a small leather case from her purse.

"Does it not occur to you, Mother, that I might want something to drink?"

"One moment, young man." Mother motioned for him not to go. "It seems my daughter does indeed care to order an alcoholic beverage." Talia could feel the explosion under thin layers of her face, the flames lapping each ear as the man stood beside her with pencil and pad and that hideous grin.

"No, I—I don't care for anything just now."

"We're ready for menus then, I believe," Mother said and withdrew eyeglasses from the case.

His smile now only half-ripe, the man pulled two menus from under an arm and dealt them with short, swift movements to his clientele.

Mother slipped the pair of half-lens eyeglasses over her nose and ran a finger down the stiff card. Her hair was pulled back in the same severe manner Talia had always known. The color had once been the same as Talia's, but when Mother began to gray it was lightened, so that now the neat twist at the nape of her neck was a warm, chestnut brown rather than black. Mother's appearance was always the same: a minimum of makeup artfully applied to accentuate classic features; hair smoothed over crown, forming a tidy diadem in back. Talia wondered if the taut pull of the coiffure had lessened the chance of wrinkles over the years, stretching porcelain skin so that lines had no opportunity to form. The thought filled her with a strange, tingling sort of fright; if the hairpins were removed the whole face might fall forward in crepey folds and lie in a heap at the base of the high cheekbones.

"The quiche is always good," Mother said.

"I don't think I'm that hungry."

"Of course you are." Mother closed the menu with finality and placed a napkin in her lap.

"Actually, I'm not terribly fond of eggs," Talia said.

"Nonsense. You love quiche lorraine."

"Mother, I'm truly not very hungry today."

"You will be." She reopened the menu and replaced her glasses, forming an inverted bridge across her nose. "Shall we have hot tea?"

"Yes, Mother, fine."

A taller, more delicate waiter came to their table, a sad insect-like mustache attempted under his nose. Mother ordered: quiche for Talia, salad for herself. She then slipped a chain from the temple of her eyeglasses and returned them to their case with long slender, comely hands. Talia had always coveted her mother's greatest beauty, these thin, graceful, artist's hands.

"You and Michael must see this Postimpressionist show. You don't like van Gogh, of course, but there's Cézanne, and Emile Bernard, and—"

"Yes, we'll try."

"Michael will be bored, no doubt. Steer him toward Gauguin and he can leer at the Tahitians for a while. You'll love Seurat; he's so precise."

"You're always critical of Michael."

"Don't be testy, I was making a joke." As Mother sipped water, light was reflected in the prismatic patterns of her glass. "They had that delightful painting by Toulouse-Lautrec you see in all the books. You know, the one of the couple dancing. You'll adore that."

"I don't like Lautrec."

"Of course you do."

"Of course, forgive me, Mother. And all this time I thought I didn't care for the man."

"I was not aware marriage gave a daughter license to be rude."

"I apologize."

"I should expect as much, I see you so rarely."

"Mother, you see me plenty."

"You've lost weight. Doesn't Michael allow groceries in that house?"

"You see? Everything is blamed on him."

"Have you been ill?"

"No."

"I've never seen you so thin. Nothing is wrong?"

"No, Mother."

A warm plate was set before Talia. An unapproachable mountain of custard rested on a ledge of pastry, and a river flowed from sliced zucchini toward the crust, slowly discoloring the lower reaches of the white cliff.

"You need to take care of yourself." Mother squeezed lemon through cheesecloth, liquid running down the crevices of torn spinach leaves. "Daddy and I were afraid of something like this."

"I've always wondered, Mother—is he your father too?"

"I don't appreciate your sarcasm, young lady. What's gotten into you?"

"Nothing."

"If you cannot speak civilly, at least eat your lunch." She gestured back to the terrain on Talia's plate.

With a fork Talia dug into the mountain, a cloud of vapor escaping as she lifted the peak. She picked up her knife and began running the blade along the inside circumference of green circles. After each revolution was completed the band of peel was lifted and removed to a separate realm. Then she cut across the diameter of each remaining smaller circle, until every orb was sliced in half.

"For the third time, Talia, what are you doing?"

"Cutting my food." Talia dissected the halves into quarters.

"Well, stop it, you're making a mess." Mother puppetized a tea bag, dunking it again and again into the steaming cup. "How are you doing in school?"

"Fine."

"You're doing well?"

"*Yes.*"

"You know that Daddy thinks you should earn a Ph.D."

"Yes, Mother, you've told me a thousand times."

"And he's right. With a doctorate you could be independent anywhere in the world. You could even join him at the university if you cared about his happiness."

"Mother, I'm not going back to Athens. I have a husband. Michael and I have a home here."

"And probably a family soon. I know Michael—I can see the glint in his eye."

"Michael's not interested in a family right now."

"He will be."

"You don't know that."

"Based on observation and comparison, believe me, I do. He's threatened, my dear. Like all men, he wants you trapped."

The lower half of the pie was a dull green sponge. Talia explored the mass with her fork, excavating bacon from the pores.

"I only mention this because I'm thinking of your career. Stop picking at your food, Talia."

"I'm through." Talia laid down her fork.

"No, you're not."

"Mother, I am."

"Finish your meal and we'll run down to Saks for a new dress. You look atrocious in those slacks."

"I don't like to try on clothes."

Mother stood and said: "I'm going to the ladies' room. Be through when I come back."

Talia ran the tines of her fork under the soggy crust and plunged the boulder to its side. With her knife she flattened the mass and then sawed the substance in half. Holding her napkin at the edge of her plate, she scraped two thirds of the devastated landscape inside and placed the leaking square of linen in a vacant chair. She pushed the remaining food from side to side, then rested the knife and fork in the center of the plate.

"That's better," Mother commented upon returning. "We must keep up your strength."

"Yes," Talia looked at Mother and smiled. "We must."

"We need size five," Mother said, as she pulled hangered selections from the rack.

Talia sat deep into the plush of a wingback chair at Saks and watched a heavy clerk waddle after Mother, the flimsy material of the woman's dress flowing like water over the wide surface of her rear.

"Let's try these on, dear," Mother said to Talia, and the broad saleswoman escorted them to an octagonal dressing room with mirrors covering each wall.

"Let's not just stand there, Talia. Get undressed." Both women stared at her, and she felt as if the room were closing in.

"I'll walk out when I'm dressed," Talia said.

"No need for that. There's plenty of room in here." Mother took a seat on a gold divan, still staring.

"I'd rather you wait outside."

"Don't be silly." Mother expelled the hanger from a dress. "Turn around and I'll unzip you."

"No! I mean—I can do it myself."

Mother walked toward her. "I always help when you try on clothes. Now turn around and let's get this done, Talia Victoria."

Talia panicked: she mustn't be seen!

"Wait outside, Mother."

"I will overlook your rudeness and newfound modesty, Talia, and ask you once again to get undressed."

"I demand my privacy," Talia said, moving back-

ward, away from Mother and the clerk, hands pressed
against mirror.

"I've never heard such nonsense."

"Leave the room, Mother!"

"What is going on here?"

Talia walked to the door: "If you don't, I will."

"I cannot *believe* what I am hearing."

"Are you going?"

"Something has come over you, young lady, and I
fully intend to discover what," Mother said, rebuffed,
as she left the room.

Now alone, Talia stood in the center of the dressing
room, slowly turning as eight counterparts circled
about. She unzipped her turtleneck and pulled the
sweater free from slacks, then crossed her arms to pull
it over her head; sixteen mirrored appendages did the
same. She raised the sweater only to her chest, a bare
stomach reflected before her. Her midriff was gro-
tesquely outspread, stretching from mirror to mirror.
She put her hands to her cheeks; too full. Currant eyes
stared back at her; eyes in eight full and ill-defined
faces. Goya images flowed hideously together; unsight-
ly skin expanded and overlapped. Talia extended a
hand to stop it and a tangle of hands, meant to strangle
and choke her, reached back. Terrified, she fumbled for
the door, finding herself wherever she looked. She
found the knob at last, and one of the eight loathsome
figures swung with her as she flung open the door.

"I'm going to be late getting home." Michael held
receiver between head and shoulder, collating stacks of
paper as he spoke.

"How long will you be?" Talia said in the crisp, lucid voice he admired.

"It shouldn't take too long. A few hours, I suppose."

"You don't want dinner?"

"No," he said, his stomach feeling as if a molten
mass. "How was your mother?"

"Will you eat?" she said.

"Yes, Talia, I'll eat. Don't wait supper." And he felt a slight twinge as he smacked into the phone and said: "Love you. I'll see you tonight."

He slid a rubber band around a stack of papers and threw them into a drawer of his desk to be filed tomorrow. He should do it now, he knew; Talia would do it now. She was a perfectionist—methodical, really—to the point of being absurd, he guessed, but he had always been proud of her compulsiveness. He had never known anyone quite as perfect as his wife. Wife; the word sounded strange to him now as he said it to himself. They had been married less than a year, but it seemed an eternity since he had felt Talia was truly his wife. When they were dating she had been so different, such an intellectual. She had introduced him to sculpture and painting and had talked of books and writers he had never heard of but pretended to know. They had quietly listened to music together by the hour and she had listened so attentively to *him*. But now she couldn't keep still long enough to thumb through a magazine, much less carry on an intelligent conversation or listen to what was happening to Michael at work. What was worse, she didn't seem to care. Or it was more as if she didn't have the capacity to care about the important things anymore. She was more like a child. But she wasn't a child! he thought and slammed the steel drawer of the desk. Even if he did go home, he rationalized now, he wouldn't see her; she'd be in the kitchen doing whatever it was she did these days with her collection of utensils and cookbooks and food she never ate.

"I'm going home now, Mr. Freeman," the words of his secretary came, interrupting his thoughts, as she stood just within his office door. "If you haven't anything else."

"That's fine, Sue," he said, then added: "Close my door when you go out."

"Yes, sir. Good night."

He waited until the clicking of her heels faded and

the doors of the building closed at the far end of the hall.

For several minutes he watched the phone, then, quickly, sat forward and put a hand to the receiver. He removed the instrument from its cradle and punched the push-button panel seven times. As the phone began to ring he leaned back again into the chair and cleared his throat.

She answered: her voice intoning the freedom of a bird.

"Carolyn?" he said. "You busy?"

3

The drive wound before him, the greens of the golf course tugging at each side, lights from the tennis courts and clubhouse coruscating beyond. Michael slowed at the security gate, the sign overhead reading "Cross Creek." He dimmed his lights and the night watchman came to the door of the gatehouse, smiled, and waved Michael through. The familiarity was like a touch of the man's hand.

Michael proceeded up the hill, rolling over speed breakers, passing building after building and rows of lighted windows; homes of people he would never know. He wound to the right, heading upward still. The parking lot in front of Carolyn's apartment was nearly full; a Volvo or Mercedes in almost every spot. He circled around the lot twice, hoping for a larger opening for his Porsche. He always tried to park diagonally across two spaces to prevent anyone from banging a door or chipping the paint. He loved this car, bought as soon as he had finished law school and been hired by a small firm in Decatur, long before he married. It was his first break with lower middle class; his emblem of having risen. The day he bought the car he drove for hours. Drove so fast and hard he felt there had been a process of cohesion during the act, his arms and legs forming a molecular attraction, becoming a part of the machine. The feeling was beyond sexual, beyond power even. The only term which correctly defined it was: ascension. That first night he had dreamt of his flight, the white Porsche carrying him over social strata and economic barriers like a stallion. But in the

26

midst of his soaring he suddenly alighted on an abandoned road, old and rugged and full of furrows. He passed miles of shabby mill houses, their wood rotting, their tin roofs rusting, and their former occupants dead. The sky began to gray, and in a fog Michael ran over something he mistook for an animal. As he stepped from the automobile to see if the creature lived, he saw the contorted face of his father, his body pinned under the wheel, his tubercular cough shaking the car. Now, he rarely thought of Pop, rationalizing over the years that success should not be a formula for guilt.

He eased the car into the one empty parking space at the far end of the asphalt lot. He picked up a bottle of Burgundy from the passenger seat, kissed the neck with a smack, and began to whistle as he put the key into the car door lock.

His breathing was short and fast as he pushed the buzzer, having climbed the steps two and three at a time. He was still bent at the waist, heaving, contemplating his knees when she came to the door. Raising his head slightly to see her, Michael walked forward in a stoop, a hand on his back, the bottle dragging the floor. "Dr. Stepler, the eminent psychiatrist, I presume?" he said.

"Nut!"

"Please. None of that professional jargon tonight."

"I'm on the phone." She smiled and motioned him in with fingers that flapped against the heel of her hand like a talking mouth.

"Wine?" He held out the bottle.

"Please."

He watched her walk in stocking feet to a table by the couch and pick up the receiver. He mentally touched her legs, slowly moving upward to the sensitive part at the back of her knees. He lingered here a moment, as he knew she would physically want him to do, then proceeded up along the smooth inside of her thighs.

"Sorry," she spoke into the mouthpiece. "Someone

at the door." Not someone; your lover, he wanted to say.

She was still dressed from work, her shoes kicked off and lying outsole to outsole, forming a heart on the carpeted floor. Scattered papers, magazines, and an open briefcase lay on the sofa; her raincoat and scarf thrown over a chair. Carolyn had a way of leaving a trail of herself as she entered a room, clothing and paraphernalia strewn about as she walked through. What amazed Michael was the way everything else was meticulously neat. No dust. No clutter. Every closet and drawer neatly organized, every article in place. It was as if someone else lived there by day and this beautiful interloper came by night to sleep, change clothes, and brush her teeth while the owners were away. She had told Michael she attributed it to the fact that she had not decorated the apartment herself but had hired a designer to come in for two weeks last summer and redo everything while she vacationed. It had cost a not-small fortune to fill the rooms with glass and chrome and hang Calders on two of the walls. Michael liked it, if not for its aesthetic value, then for its price. Carolyn said it left her cold.

She sat on the sofa with the phone in her lap. Her legs were crossed at the ankle and rested on a glass-topped table, polished nails showing a dark red through nylons.

Michael removed a corkscrew from a drawer of the liquor cabinet and fastened it over the bottle. The cork was dry and began to crumble as he began to screw. No good; he tried again. This time the stopper was pushed into the wine and particles of cork floated in the liquid.

"Damn!"

Carolyn shushed him with a raised hand without looking his way. Forget the wine. He took a bar glass from an upper shelf, Carolyn's three initials etched in the crystal. Carolyn Thames Stepler. Thames was the name her mother used; a maiden name, Michael assumed. He had never gotten the entire story, but apparently her parents, both doctors like herself, had separated when Carolyn was three. Her mother practiced psychiatry in New Jersey, where she and Carolyn had lived; her estranged father practiced medicine in New York. Occasionally, on weekends, her father would come in from his city apartment and they would return to family status for a short while. "It's a perfect situation," Carolyn had told Michael when they first met. "They're both independent, industrious, intelligent people. They care for each other, certainly, but do not need each other, or anyone else for that matter, to survive."

Michael poured Scotch into the glass and then walked to the kitchen for ice. He ran a finger along the bottom of Carolyn's foot as he passed and she kicked playfully at his hand. When he returned to the living room he walked behind the sofa with his drink. Carolyn's head rested on the back of the couch, her hair a glowing contrast against the upholstery's dark brown. Michael bent over her, sliding hands down the length of her arms, nestling his head in her gold mane. It was thick and noticeably coarse compared to Talia's baby-fine hair.

"No, I enjoyed it. You didn't disturb a thing." Like hell, Michael thought. "Glad you called, Charles." He heard the receiver go down; she had a thing against saying good-bye. She returned the phone to the table from her lap and leaned her neck backward to see Michael. He studied this inverted view of her mouth: the bottom lip was full and slightly wet, the top consisting of two curving arcs forming a perfect V. A few freckles were sprinkled over her nose; beautiful, independent, camus nose. He ran a finger over its bridge and along the curve of its bow.

"How are you?" she said softly.

"Terrible. Work's killing me and my wife's flipping out. Care to hear what she did last night?"

"No."

"I wish you could have seen her at our party," said Michael. "Want a drink?"

"I thought we were having wine."

"I crumbled my cork. You smell good." He pressed against her ear. "Who's Charles?"

"A good friend."

"How good?" He began nibbling her lobe.

"Good."

"But *how* good?"

"He called to discuss a case."

"New dress?" He played with the top button. "It looks great," he said. The dress was expensive, he knew, and fit her perfectly, accentuating all the parts of her body he admired. "Man, it's good to be here. Carolyn, you should have seen her. I swear she's cracking up."

Carolyn leaned forward, picking up magazines and papers from the sofa, stacking them inside a Plexiglas rack. Closing her briefcase, she carried it to her desk. She had a habit of becoming fanatically neat when she was irritated or something was wrong.

"Sure you wouldn't like a drink?" he ventured.

"Positively." She picked her shoes off the rug and walked with them to her bedroom.

"Okay, what did I say?"

"You know the trouble with being the other woman? You begin to be treated like a wife. And I intend to be no one's wife!"

"Hey."

"You may be the oligarch at home, but not around here."

"Crap, Carolyn. What's that supposed to mean?"

"I don't like being your counselor. When I come home the office is closed."

"Understood."

"At the end of a day I'm sick of interpreting the idiosyncrasies of a spouse."

He put his arms around her, letting one hand rub up and down her back. "May I come out of the corner now?"

She pulled away and sat. "I do not intend to be taken for granted, Mike."

"I never intended that you should." He sat beside her now on the bed and began kneading her thigh. "I apologize," he said. "Don't be mad."

"Then don't treat me like a wife, ever."

The sheets were cool and clean, smelling faintly of Carolyn.

Michael ran his hand along the slope of her smooth, well-toned stern. There was a distinct difference between the white, sacred skin of her buttocks and the remainder of last summer's tan.

He had once, several years ago, made a rafting trip down the Chattooga River. There had been fear, terror almost, in this sort of horizontal free-fall with the water. He had worked his tail off to keep the raft out of danger, to keep from cutting too swiftly or falling too soon. But at the end of the ride he experienced a sensation of control; he had succeeded in something few men were able to do and therefore overpowered them. This frightening thrill was his metaphor for satisfying Carolyn; for keeping his lover.

With his finger he traced the outline of her spine and kissed the small of her back. "I've got to go," he said.

She propped herself against pillows and held her knees to her chest as he dressed before a mirror. "You're narcissistic, Mike."

"All men love their bodies. You're the psychiatrist, you should know that." He stuffed his shirttail into his pants.

"But not as blatantly as you." She picked up his eyeglasses from the nightstand. "Here, don't forget your affectation." Each time before making love, it was she, not he, who removed them and placed them on the stand.

Carolyn walked with him to the door, still nude, her stomach athletically flat, her breasts firm without support. He stroked the white fluff which ran vertically to her navel, then cupped his hands over her breasts as he kissed her good-bye.

"Be careful driving home," she said. "I would despise looking for a replacement."

"I doubt that would be so difficult." He wanted to hear the opposite.

"But it would," she grinned. "You satisfy all the criteria. Not only do I adore your body, my dear, you're also safely married."

Michael's key sounded in the door.

Talia quickly returned the telephone receiver to its hook and turned to meet him. "Where have you been?" she said when he walked inside.

"You know where I've been."

"I called the office."

"So?" He unloosened his tie and plopped his brief-case down on the kitchen table.

"No one answered."

"The switchboard closes after five. You know that."

"I was afraid something had happened. It was getting so late."

"Christ! Talia, it's only nine thirty."

She followed him to the living room. "Where's the paper?" he said as he flicked on the TV.

"No one knew where you were."

"No one *what?*"

"I called everywhere."

"You mean you've been calling around trying to find me?"

"I tried Harrison's and that bar at the Omni."

"Damn, Talia."

"Frank said you go there sometimes."

"You called Stoner? Shit, Talia, I have problems enough without you embarrassing me like this."

"I was worried."

"Worry less, would you?" He walked past her, tie in hand.

"You've been drinking."

"I'm going to bed."

"I thought you said you were working."

"I keep a bottle of Scotch in my desk drawer. Second down on the right. Any more questions?"

"Did you get much done?"

"Not as much as I would have liked."

Talia was alone now; empty; as if someone had died.

She was miserable when Michael angered this way, and Michael angered often these days. He was continuously upset; he and Mother and Father. But it had always been this way; even as a child; it was always Talia the mediator, bearing the burden of peace. In those days it was Allyson who always upset things, who spilled her watercolors and left papers on the floor, who refused to do as she was told. And it was always Talia who ran behind her, cleaning, straightening, making things all right again, making certain there would be no disagreements and that Mother and Father would not lash out at one another; especially after Allyson's death. But she tried not to think of that now, tried not to remember; there was too much guilt involved with death. One was always having to make up for someone's pain. It was Talia who had had to make it up to Father and Mother. It was always Talia, even now, even with Michael. Only the burden was becoming heavier and heavier, more weighty than Talia could bear. They all wanted her to do the correct thing, yet she didn't know what the correct thing was. They expected things of her she wasn't able to do. Possibly she wasn't capable of doing anything. Possibly she was nothing; a faceless blur reshaped periodically like a drift of sand.

She opened the refrigerator, pulling cartons from the freezer compartment. It was their problem, she thought. She had no way of knowing what they wanted. She had no control over what made them angry; she had no control.

She put two cardboard containers on the kitchen table and opened them, carefully, one at a time. The colors were delicious: alizarin crimson and deep velvet brown. The red was the color of Michael when he angered. The brown the color of Mother's maid, Clara, the one who had made sugar cookies when Talia was a child. She was consuming Clara. She was destroying Michael's face.

"Talia? What the hell are you doing?"

She hadn't heard him!

"Talia, there's ice cream all over the place."

She scooped up the cartons and ran with them to the sink. She must hurry! Mustn't let him see!

"You've got that stuff all over your robe. Talia, what's going on here?"

"Nothing!"

"You haven't eaten all this, have you?"

"Go away!"

"Talia, what have you been doing? There are two empty half-gallons of ice cream here."

"Go away!" She ran from the kitchen to the bathroom and locked the door. She could still hear Michael above the pounding water as she turned on the shower and rotated the handles at the sink.

"Talia, what are you doing in there?"

Flushing the commode, she stood and opened the medicine cabinet. She took a box from the shelf and filled a glass with water.

"Talia, what's going on! Are you sick?"

The directions on the package said to take one tablet before retiring. Talia placed three in her mouth and swallowed, following the laxatives with only a fourth of the liquid.

"I demand that you open this door!" Michael hammered it with his fist as Talia returned the package to the cabinet and then splashed water over her face.

"What were you doing in there?"

"Nothing."

"What's going on?"

"Stop asking me that."

She went to the exercise bicycle Michael had given her and set the timer for fifteen minutes. She was behind today; she must fit this in.

"Talia, get off that thing and talk to me."

She pushed the pedals harder and harder, the wheels turning against the resistance of a disc of rubber.

"Talia, I don't understand."

Good! For once it was Michael who didn't comprehend.

"Go to bed, Michael," Talia said. "I need my exercise."

4

Ambivalence stirred within Talia as she and Michael reached her parents' drive.

She had not visited their home since summer; live oaks surrounding the house had shed during her absence, making it appear undressed and more unapproachable than ever. The house was a sprawling monster that spread spasmodically over the lawn and sank into boxwood and monkey grass, showing no foundation; no end. Ivy climbed the white brick wall and effected a porous screen across the half-moon window which fanned out over the massive front door. On the side of the house, James's basketball ring still circled above the opening to the garage; the net had disintegrated and only a rusty loop lingered behind. Talia used to watch him practice here, his laughs ringing above them each time he bucketed a shot. James had been the oldest, the best. He was Mother's favorite and had been good at everything—everything except getting along with Father. Talia used to have to come between them, try to pacify each of them, the same way she knew she would try with Father and Michael today. James had been like Michael in some ways: the same age, same size, same character which grated on Father; the same kind of wit which Talia enjoyed but which Father regarded as flippant and rude. Talia had loved James, had wanted to be like him; as a child she had copied the way he walked, tried to mimic his smile, his laugh, the way he dressed. She had wanted to be a man. She still did sometimes—when she thought of his death—still wished she could have gone to war as he did, could have rebelled against Father and died the pure, brave death of a soldier and then been grieved over for years by Mother. But she wasn't a man. She wasn't James. She was a cross between what the world believed her to be and what she couldn't become; she was half of nothing.

"I don't want to stay all day, Talia. We'll go in; have lunch; and say we have another engagement in Atlanta tonight," Michael said.

"It's only one day, Michael. One day out of the year."

"One too many. I've been dreading this for weeks."

"Don't be hostile, Michael, please."

"I think I'm being pretty damn gracious considering I'll spend the next few hours being either lectured or ignored."

"Don't say that."

"Why? That's exactly what he'll do."

"You misinterpret Father."

"He's an egocentric and obstinate old man."

"You don't understand him, Michael. Father is intelligent; his mind surpasses most men's. And, in his own way, he's truly kind."

"That's your opinion, I have mine. Pick up your goodies and let's get this over with."

Talia stood outside the car and removed covered dishes from the floorboard of the Porsche. As she leaned to pick up the last one, a platter fell from her hands to the seat.

"Oh, Michael," she said and she felt the paralyzing kind of fear she had known when she had made mistakes as a child.

"What happened?" He walked around to her side of the car.

"I spilled the yams."

"In my car?"

"They were prefectly glazed."

"On the seat? Stand back." Michael pushed her away from the door. "Ah, damn!"

"It'll be okay. Mother'll probably have more."

"I don't give a damn about your stupid potatoes. Look at my car. Hold this!" Michael gave her the fallen casserole and began throwing vegetables into the dish, syrup dripping from his hands. "Damn, what a mess."

Talia ran behind him as he stalked to the front door. "Don't go charging in, Michael. At least say hello. Remember to speak to Father."

"How'd you drop it, anyway?" He leaned against the buzzer with his shoulder."

"It slipped."

"All over my car. I'll never get all that stuff up."

Mother answered the buzzer; she stood before the door like the smooth, clean surface of a porcelain plate.

"Happy Thanksgiving, Joan."

"You're dripping, Michael. Talia, come in."

"I'd give you a hug, Joan, but I have syrup on my hands."

"What happened this time?"

"It was my fault, Mother."

"Um."

"Your little girl dropped sweet potatoes all over the seat of my car. Think I could borrow a towel or a sponge?"

"Yams. I'll see what I can find," Mother said, looking disgustedly at Michael's hands. "Watch the carpet." Then to Talia: "Your father's in the library, Talia Victoria," and she pointed down the hall.

Michael still stood in the doorway after Mother was gone. "Go on in, Michael. Father's waiting," Talia said.

"Not until I get that seat clean."

"At least go in and speak to him, Michael. He'll be offended."

"You speak to him. He's your father. And besides, you wouldn't want me to get anything on *Mother's* carpet, now would you?"

Without Michael, Talia walked through the foyer to the library. Father stood at the fireplace, his back to her, a foot upon the hearth. He had the body of an athlete; sinewy arms and thighs. A perfect specimen of Man.

"Hello, Father."

He tapped his pipe against the fireplace brick before turning.

"No husband?"

"I overturned a casserole in the Porsche. Michael's cleaning it; afraid it might ruin the seat." She attempted a laugh. "You know how he loves that car."

" 'The materialist is a Calvinist without a God.' Take off your coat." She removed the jacket he had given her last Christmas. It was heavy and bulky and made her feel like a bear.

"I've loved the coat, Father. It's perfect for this weather."

"Your Michael isn't very mannerly, is he?" Father said.

"I'm sorry, Father. He—"

"Behavior does not preclude what is in the mind. The idiot might appear brilliant, or conversely, the genius might behave in an idiotic manner. It would be unfair to judge Michael, not knowing what goes on in the private realm of his mind. The self can be aware of nothing but its own experiences. What's that called?"

"Solipsism, I think?"

"Your mind hasn't gone completely to wrack since you've been from home. How are your grades?"

"Fine, sir. So far." It felt as if something were ripping the chords in her throat.

"Are you giving thought to your doctorate?"

"Yes, sir. It seems a good idea."

"Aristotle said the educated are as much superior to the uneducated as the living are to the dead."

"Yes, sir."

Michael's and Mother's footsteps sounded in the hall. Michael entered first, going directly to Father, his hand outstretched, face full of the smile he used when with older men.

"Good to see you, Dr. Sinclaire. You look well."

"That, young man, is because I *am* well."

"I apologize for being late. We had a mess out there. Talia told you, I suppose."

Father placed another log on the fire. "We were discussing Talia's education."

"I've been wanting to talk with you about that," said Michael.

"I assume you want her to continue."

"If it's best for Talia."

"Of course it's best for Talia," Mother broke in. "Louis would not have suggested it if it weren't."

Michael said, "But I believe it should be Talia's decision."

"Of course it should be Talia's decision." Mother's words were directed at Michael. "And her decision is, she wants to go."

"Do you, Talia?" Michael looked at her for the first time since entering the room.

She turned from Michael to Father to Mother, trying to judge the expression on each face. Father's was the least telling of the three. As he filled his pipe with tobacco, he spoke as if to himself: " 'Only the educated are free.' "

"But the education isn't," said Michael. "That's what I want to talk with you about, Professor."

"What's there to discuss?"

"I think it's time I started paying Talia's tuition."

"I'm her father. I pay."

"Yes, sir, but we're married now, and I think I should be responsible for Talia."

"I gave James an education. If Allyson had lived I would have provided her with one. I will do the same for my youngest."

"But I should be the one who—"

" 'He that hath wife and children hath given hostages to fortune; for they are impediments to great enterprises, either of virtue or mischief.' Do you read Francis Bacon?"

"No, sir. But I don't see what—"

"What *do* you read?"

"Well, I'm kept pretty busy at work these days."

" 'Books rule the world.' Who said that, Talia?"

"Voltaire."

" 'Books rule the world,' said Voltaire, 'or at least those nations which have a written language; the others do not count.' "

Michael jiggled coins in his pockets while muscles contracted and relaxed at his temples and above his jaw.

"We've brought you both gifts," Talia essayed to change the course of conversation. She removed two small packages from a paper bag and handed the smallest of the two to Mother.

"Conté," said Mother, taking the box of French crayons. "Aren't you kind? We raised a thoughtful daughter. Louis, didn't we raise an extraordinarily thoughtful daughter?"

"We did a good job." Father leaned against the fireplace, the smoke from his pipe ascending and forming a nimbus about his head. He smiled at Talia and, for a moment, she thought he might invite an embrace.

"And yours, Father, is a biography of Hoffer."

"Hoffer." He unwrapped the package and turned the book in his hands. "Have you read anything by this man?"

"No, sir."

"Then you're not familiar with his philosophies?"

"Not truly." Dampness poured onto Talia's palms.

"Eric Hoffer would consider me intelligentsia, with a bitter taste in his mouth." Father handed the book to Talia.

"I could exchange it for something else."

"I don't agree with everything I read. Put it down."

"Yes, sir," Talia said, stung. "I'll carry our coats upstairs."

From the second floor Talia could hear Michael and Father discussing her education and the money. Michael emphatically believed it was now his duty to pay for everything that was hers. It was an affront to him, Talia knew, to have Father paying her tuition to graduate school, as much as it would be an affront for Father to surrender the responsibility to Michael. Father had always given her everything; given her more than she could prove herself worthy of. And now, with Michael, she was obligated to prove herself worthy of the giving of two.

She closed the door of her childhood room against the voices and threw the coats on the same azure comforter that had always lain across the bed. Nothing had changed here: same blue chintz curtains on the windows (with their print of the captured unicorn tied to the pomegranate tree), same canopy on the bed, same painting on the wall. The painting was one Mother had copied from Monet's *The River*. The perspective was off and Mother had never understood the theory of color—so the landscape appeared as if it were turned inside out.

The shelves over her desk were empty now, and a zigzagging line of dust showed where her books had been. She knew by heart where each would go; knew exactly where each fit inside the outline of dust. First Austen, then the Brontës, the Brownings, Dickinson, and Eliot all on the first row. She blew dust from the shelves; Mother was no better with housekeeping than she was with color.

She waited here a minute more, running her fingers over the quilting of the comforter. There was something about this room, like the rest of the house, which made her want to stay forever and at the same instant caused her to want to find Michael and run away.

The other three were seated at the dining room table as Talia stirred sauce for peas.

"Has she seen a doctor?" It was Mother's voice.

"I haven't really seen a need," said Michael.

"But she's too thin."

"She's on a diet."

"I see no need for vexation, Joan." It was Father now. "She's inherited my self-control."

"But Louis, she's gaunt. She looks like some war-ravaged German Käthe Kollwitz would have drawn."

" 'No work of art is worth the bones of a Pomeranian Grenadier.' " Father laughed at this.

"Louis, I'm concerned!"

"Talk to Michael. He likes to think he's in charge of things now."

"Michael? What do you think?"

"I think she's probably overdone the diet, but she's physically fine."

"Well, I don't like it. She should have a checkup. She hasn't seen Dr. Abelard since she married."

Talia was sorry the topic changed as she entered the room.

"You've prepared enough for an army, dear." Mother helped with the vessels Talia carried. "I just can't get excited about Thanksgiving anymore. We used to have wonderful holidays when James was still alive, didn't we? You remember."

"Yes, Mother."

"You were here, weren't you, Michael? That year before he died."

"No, ma'am. I wasn't here."

"He was so happy that last year. So full of life."

Father clanked an iced-tea spoon against a glass as if he were about to propose a toast. "You played football, didn't you, Michael?"

"Uh, no, sir."

"All my children were athletic. Talia ranked number one on the city tennis team for two years." Father turned to her. "Do you play in Atlanta?"

"I practice against a backboard quite often."

"But you don't play?"

"No, sir."

"That's a large investment to throw away with lassitude, Talia Victoria."

"How are things at school, Professor?" said Michael. Talia wished she could thank him for that.

"As compared to what?" said Father.

"I mean—are your classes going well?"

"As well as can be expected with the caliber of students we have. 'Upon the education of the people of this country the fate of this country depends.' Who said that, Michael?"

"I haven't the faintest."

"Talia?"

"Disraeli?"

"Hah! I taught you well. 'We have fought this war and won it. Now let us not be sanctimonious; nor hypocritical; nor vengeful; nor stupid. Let us make our enemies incapable of ever making war again, let us re-educate them, . . . but first we must educate ourselves.' " Father was almost out of his chair as he spoke, his hand upraised in a fist. "Who, Talia Victoria?"

She affected a chew and swallowed nothing from an empty mouth. "Hemingway?"

He slammed his fist against the table. "Good girl!"

"James loved Hemingway. His favorite writer." Mother dabbed at her eyes with a napkin. "He read *A Farewell to Arms* four times."

"He read it twice, Joan. And that was because he didn't get it the first time."

"That's unfair. You resent him because he wasn't a philosopher like you."

"It was his life. I never interfered."

"No, but you never treated him as well as you did the girls."

"Would anyone care for more tea?" Talia's stomach wreathed as she stood.

"Don't be jumping up and down at the table, child. Everyone is fine. Your mother becomes lachrymose when she has ham."

"How can you be so insensitive about his death?" Mother accused.

"Freud said that the goal of all life is death. I cannot be maudlin about something as simple as that."

Talia stared at Michael, begging him to interject. He glanced her way and coughed uncomfortably.

"And how is *your* work?" Father placed another slice of ham on Michael's plate.

"Actually it couldn't be better, sir. We're working on a new—"

"I could get you a job in town."

Michael put down his fork. "Excuse me?"

"I have connections. Good friends who are attorneys. With a word or two I could get you in."

"Thank you, but I *don't think*—"

"As soon as Talia gets her doctorate she could come back here and teach."

Michael's face was a twisted red beet.

"Father, I—"

"And it would make things easier on her mother. Talia is all we have left."

"You're not that far from Atlanta. I think we can all manage fine." Michael pushed his chair from the table. Father saw the movement and stood first.

"Everyone may be excused if you like. Joan, shall we have coffee by the fire?"

While Mother was upstairs (it was her custom after meals; she would return a few minutes later, Talia knew, perfumed and with fresh lipstick on her lips) Talia quickly cleared the table so no one would notice her plate had remained untouched. Carefully she removed her uneaten food and returned it to the refrigerator; she returned to the library as her secret cooled.

"Ah, Talia!" Father said. "You should teach your Michael something of chess. Come. Play me a game."

Michael stood by the fire, hands clenched at his sides, resembling the rounded tops of upturned pawns.

"I'd best not, Father. It's getting late and we have another engagement tonight."

"I should think you could stay. It's one day out of the year." Talia and Michael resisted exchanging looks.

"Yes, sir. We hate to go, but it's unavoidable, I'm afraid."

"You have your own lives. You know what you must do."

Father assisted her with her coat and touched her cheek with his hand as he said good-bye. " 'To go is to die a little.' Who said it, my dear?"

"Rupert Brooke, Father."

"I did teach you well." He kissed her forehead after the praise. She could still feel the touch as she and Michael were in the car.

"God, I hate that man!"

"Please, Michael. Don't."

"Christmas we're staying home. Do you understand?"

"Michael, he's my father."

"I thought I would scream if I heard another word. Where does he get all that crap?"

"He reads."

"He's so condescending he makes me ill. And your Mother, my God."

"She doesn't do that often."

"She does when I'm around."

Talia touched the glass of the window at her side, leaving a damp impression when she removed her hand. She had wanted to do this all day; reach out and touch the glass that surrounded her and kept her from the others.

"All his stupid quotations and your knowing who said what!"

"It's a game."

"It's absurd."

"James and Allyson would never play."

"Yeah, well they were smart. Your mother thinks you're sick. She says you're too thin."

"But I'm not."

"She thinks you are. I think it. You are!"

Mother goes on diets."

"Well, she apparently doesn't want you on one and neither do I."

"It's not her body."

"It may not be but she's going to bug me just the same." He faced her. "Did you eat?"

She turned and pressed her face against the glass and spoke the word without a tremor: "Yes."

= 5 =

They walked along the right-hand side of the corridor toward the Coastal Airlines gates. A large standing ashcan had been overturned, and sand and cigarette butts were strewn over the concrete floor.

"You're sure you're going to be okay?" Michael said to Talia.

"Do you think we should pick that up?" she said.

"And have some poor slob lose his job?" He held her arm as they stepped over the can. "You have plenty of money, right?"

Talia nodded, still looking over her shoulder at the scattered mess.

"And I left you enough checks?"

"Someone might slip and fall. Hurt themselves."

"Stop worrying about the world, Talia. You have the name of the guy to call in case the Audi doesn't start?"

"Yes."

She seemed particularly vulnerable to Michael today, almost a child, as she hurried along beside him, taking several steps to keep pace with his one. She looked waifed; outfitted in last year's clothes, which now hung from her shoulders and bunched about her where she had cinched them at the waist.

"You remember what to do if you blow a fuse?"

"Yes, Michael."

"There's a flashlight in the drawer."

"I remember, Michael."

At gate eleven he instructed Talia to take a seat while he waited in line. Before the ticket counter he searched the crowd. A weary-looking woman held a

48

baby, rocking him back and forth in the plastic chair; a slightly older child crawled at her feet, a paste of saliva and saltines plastered over his clothing and stuck to his hands. Businessmen and salesmen lined one wall, their heads pressed against painted concrete blocks, each, like the blocks, homologous with one another in their slick, polyester suits.

Scanning, Michael found her: a blond oasis along this banal human tract. She was seated behind Talia, a row away; her face downturned, she was barely visible from where Michael stood.

The line moved forward and the agent said good afternoon and spoke Michael's name as he stamped the ticket. Michael looked to see if Carolyn had overheard; her head remained bent over an issue of *Scientific American*, unconcerned. The airline employee stapled the boarding pass and returned the ticket to Michael: "Have a nice flight, Mr. Freeman," the man said. Michael glanced again toward Carolyn. She still looked down.

"Thank you. I will." Michael spoke too loudly, hoping she would respond to his voice. Only Talia looked his way.

He slipped the ticket inside the breast pocket of his suit coat and walked to his wife. His guilt was not so much for leaving her, or even for being with Carolyn on this trip, but for being ashamed of the way Talia looked. But damn it! if she had only dressed nicely this once. Here she was so close to Carolyn they could easily touch and she looked utterly impoverished with those clothes and unkempt hair and dark circles under her eyes.

"The plane leaves in ten minutes," he spoke almost in whispers now. "You don't have to stay if you don't want."

"I don't mind."

"You're sure you can manage everything? You have the number in Miami? The name of the hotel?"

"Yes, Michael. I'll be fine."

"If anything happens you can run to the Carlyles next door."

"Nothing will happen."

"I left you plenty of cash, right?"

"Yes, Michael. I told you that."

The blare of Muzak was broken as a voice crackled over the speaker and Michael's flight was announced. Carolyn walked to the gate, never once looking his way, and found a position at the front of the line.

"Okay!" He almost laughed as he said it. "Guess this is it. I'll see you in a week." He kissed Talia on the forehead and took the newspaper she had held. "You're sure you'll be all right?"

"Yes, fine. Have a good meeting."

He could see the red and gold of Carolyn out of the corner of his eye as she walked up the ramp. Practicalities pulled him to the ground while the rest of him wanted to fly. "You have everything you need, don't you?"

"I have what I need. I love you—Michael."

"Me too."

Talia waved as he ran after Carolyn, the tiny outline of her lone hand silhouetted against the airport wall.

Michael squeezed down the aisle of the plane, brushing the backs of fellow travelers as they placed articles overhead. They all seemed comrades now, having risen above the platitudinous waiting room. As he pushed through, he thought he could see the glint of her head. Yes! that was her; to the right; by the window. He wanted to call to Carolyn; climb over seats; bash people in the head with his attaché case.

He bumped against an elderly woman: "Excuse me," and as he bent to help her secure her paper-bag luggage, he could see Carolyn fully, her face cool as she surveyed the airplane's wing through the glass.

A scrawny boy with acne and wiry hair and a guitar fastened over his shoulder hesitated at the empty seat next to Carolyn's. "No, man! Keep going!" Michael wanted to say.

Someone called to the boy from the rear of the plane

as he reached behind himself to remove the guitar. He shrugged at Carolyn, they both smiled, and he then proceeded down the aisle, the instrument still tied to his back.

Michael pushed his briefcase under the seat in front of him as he sat. Carolyn was facing the window again, seemingly oblivious to his presence. She was so near he could smell the scent of shampoo which lingered in her hair.

He cleared his throat; Carolyn leaned back in her chair; she fastened her seat belt; he executed a self-conscious yawn. Not until the plane rolled free of the building and began to taxi safely from the eyes of Atlanta did he touch her, pulling back the slightly scented hair from her face.

Carolyn sat curled on the bed. A silk robe was pulled about her and her hair was still pinned from their bath. A few strands had pulled free and curled damply on her neck.

Michael stood naked beside her, the hotel's monogrammed towel neatly folded over his arm. He twirled the bottle of champagne between his hands in the bucket of ice.

"Champagne, madame?"

"By all means."

The cork hit the wall and Michael tried to catch the overflow in two plastic glasses. "My cup runneth over," he said.

"And so does your mouth." She laughed.

He wiped the sides and bottom of each cup with his towel and presented Carolyn with the wine. "Will there be anything more?" he said with a dramatic bow.

"I don't think I could stand any more."

They had been seeing each other now for months, and yet, he was nervous. Each time he thought he was beginning to know Carolyn, he learned quite quickly he was wrong. There was a physical closeness, an intimacy in her touch, but she erected a mental barrier whenever he strayed from business or sex and ventured too close.

"Then, if I may propose a toast." He raised the plastic in the air, and touched the rim of Carolyn's glass to his. "To a beautiful, marvelous, sexy week."

"I fear our sojourn may not be quite as simple as that." She sipped champagne. "I have sessions from seven to nine almost every night."

"Tell me something." He joined her on the bed. "Do you really enjoy this? I mean working on theoretical cases instead of real patients."

"You don't get involved with theoretics. Besides, it's fairly interesting and when it's not, it's a change of scenery."

"But is it really worth it to be away from your practice for a whole week?"

"My retainer specifies that I'll be out of the office a certain number of days a year. It's lucrative—I'm satisfied with that."

"And what exactly does Coastlines get out of you in return for all that cold, hard cash?"

"Initially, the profile on hijackers. And I've now been assigned to assist the ad agency in generating business for this Miami-to-London flight."

"Well, I hope you don't generate much."

"We will. Assuming the board and all the government agencies approve."

"I'm opposed to that leg."

"Better not let Frank Stoner hear you say that. He intends to ride this thing all the way to a position on the board."

"Yeah, well, he may have a tough time of it from what I hear." Michael poured himself more wine. "He's a loudmouthed fool."

"I grant you, he's gauche. But Frank is no fool."

"Maybe. But there are enough people at the top just waiting to oust him if he makes a few wrong moves."

"And you're hoping he does?"

He was glad she asked. "You could say that."

"You want his job pretty badly, don't you?"

"Damn right."

"Think you have a good chance?"

"Do you?" He searched her face; as usual it was an abyss.

"The thing that may hold you back is your age. You're young to be chief legal counsel for an airline."

"Possibly; but Frank talks too much. Hopefully they'll tire of hearing about his twenty-one-year-old honey, and forget that I'm thirty-two."

"And what happens if they discover *you* have a paramour, dear Mike?"

"They won't." He took a long swallow of the wine. "Like you say, I'm safely married. They all know I have a legitimate, respectable little wife at home who's going to hold my hand down the path to success."

He wasn't certain if it was the statement or the wine which burned his mouth.

The meeting had been going on all morning. Cigar and cigarette smoke was clouding the air. Limp paper cups and deluged ashtrays littered the conference room.

For the last ten minutes Michael had been giving one of the most important reports of his career, and everything was going exactly as planned. He sipped cold coffee from a wilted cup and started again, slowly, deliberately, emphasizing each remark with a hand striking perpendicularly across the edge of the table.

"Coastal's legal liability and the cost of insurance, coupled with depreciation of equipment, and man-hours involved for the money earned, simply do not justify taking on this one international route."

"Good God, Michael!" The table vibrated as Frank Stoner rose and pounded it with his fist. "You're acting like a kid in law school. Even worse, you sound like an accountant; you can't see past your decimal point, my boy." With an encompassing glance, Frank addressed the others in the room: "I think Michael's problem is, he hasn't been out of academia long enough to fully recognize the pragmatics of the real world. He doesn't quite seem to realize we're trying to run a business here."

Michael's face was inflamed; it was Frank who had requested this report! Frank had edited it! And now, it was Frank who stomped about the room feigning anger.

"Michael has edified us all with his graphs and statistics, his talk of liability. But he has failed to mention the very positive side of this project, which far outweighs the negative. This Miami-to-London flight will make Coastlines an international airline. The ramifications are endless. This leg could be the first big step in making Coastal one of the most powerful airlines in the world! And I don't think any classroom jargon justifies not going ahead with it."

Michael shuffled the pages of his report, fixing his eyes on a heavy glass ashtray before him to keep from looking at the adversary. Damn Frank Stoner! His overwhelming urge was to hurl the ashtray at the man.

"This company didn't get where it is today by sitting back, as Michael would have us do, being afraid to take risks. If we don't act now, someone else will. This route could be the most important—ah, damn! What now?"

Frank opened the conference-room door roughly: "Yes, what is it?" He snatched a piece of paper from an invisible messenger behind the door and walked to the table. "Beautiful timing, my boy!" He thrust the folded note at Michael and stood behind him as he read.

"It's an emergency phone call," Michael said.

"Christ, man! What is this? Don't they know you're in a meeting right now?"

"Give the man a break," someone said.

And someone else: "It's an emergency, Stoner."

"Yeah." Frank's tone changed as he slapped Michael's shoulder. "Yeah, hope it's not serious, son."

In the hall a porter gave Michael the phone.

"Yes, this is he," he responded to the operator.

"Michael?"

"Joan, what is it?"

"I didn't disturb you, I hope."

"What's happened?"

"I hear the weather is bad. What a pity to be in Miami when it's raining."

"For God's sake, Joan! What's wrong? Is it Talia?" There was complete silence on the other end of the line. "Joan, I didn't mean to shout. But I'm very, very busy right now."

"Well, if you're so busy—"

"No, I didn't mean it that way. What is it?"

"It's Talia."

"What about Talia? Has there been an accident?"

"No."

"Is she ill?"

"I don't know."

"Damn it, Joan! Would you tell me what's going on?"

"I am not accustomed to profanity, Michael Freeman."

"Joan, thirty executives are holding up a meeting for me."

"She doesn't look well."

"You called long distance to tell me she doesn't look well?"

"It's obvious I should not have phoned." Her words slid into the aristocratic, diphthonging slur he despised. "You apparently are not concerned."

"I am concerned, Joan." He looked at his watch. "What do you mean, she doesn't look well?"

"We met for lunch yesterday."

"I'm listening."

"Michael, she's lost a great deal more weight. Possibly ten or fifteen pounds."

"She couldn't have lost that much in a week."

"I tell you she *has*. I know my daughter. And she isn't acting right."

Michael heard the door of the conference room

open. Frank stepped into the hall, jabbed a finger at his watch and stomped back in.

"I insist she see a physician, even if I have to drive to Atlanta and take her myself."

"That won't be necessary. I'll see that she goes," Michael said.

"Immediately?"

"I'll be home tomorrow. I'll take care of it then."

"I want her to go to Dr. Abelard here in Athens."

"Fine."

"I can do it if you're busy."

"I'll see that she goes, Joan."

"You won't forget?"

"I said, I'll take care of it."

He immediately dialed his number in Atlanta when their connection broke.

"Talia, damn it, how do you feel?" he said as soon as she answered the phone."

"I feel fine, Michael. What's wrong?"

"Your mother called a few minutes ago."

"At the hotel?"

"Of course at the hotel. In the middle of a meeting."

"But why?"

"She thinks there's something wrong with you. Thinks you're ill. Says you've lost more weight."

There was silence.

"She wants you to go to a doctor."

"She said that before."

"Well, this time you're going. I've got to get that woman off my back."

"What else did she say?"

"We'll discuss it tomorrow. I haven't time right now. Do you have the flight number?"

She mumbled something he took as yes.

"The plane gets in at four fifteen. Leave around three to allow yourself plenty of time."

"All right, Michael." And then: "I'm sorry."

"So am I."

Michael re-entered the conference room. It was Frank who first returned to his place at the long wooden table. "Maybe now we can get through with this," Frank said, "and get out of this smoke pit for a drink."

"I apologize for the interruption." Michael took a seat.

"Everything all right?" Stoner said.

"Yes."

"Nothing serious, I hope."

"No. It was nothing. Everything is fine."

6

Michael and Carolyn deplaned together. Their flight had been behind schedule when they left Miami and they were twenty minutes late arriving in Atlanta. They emerged through the tunnel the airline used for joining building to plane, and reached the entrance gate. Michael inspected the faces in the crowd for Talia's, then turned to Carolyn: "Why don't you go ahead?" he said. "I'll call you tomorrow."

"Come on, walk with me awhile. Our liaison is almost over."

Carolyn chatted beside him as he scanned the length of the corridor, examining each face for any sign of Talia.

"Don't look so nervous," Carolyn said. "As soon as you see her, I'll run."

"I'm not nervous. Just curious. She's like her father, never late."

"Well, maybe she forgot."

"Talia doesn't forget."

"Oh, par*don*."

The conveyor belt moved through the room like a giant serpent with parasites of luggage feeding on its back. Michael placed his briefcase on the scuffed terminal floor and pulled his and Carolyn's bags free of the belt. He placed Carolyn's on a cart and gave a porter some change.

"I can take care of my own tips, thanks." She placed a dollar in Michael's hand. "Come on," she smiled. "I'll give you a ride."

"I'd love it, but she's probably waiting upstairs."

"You sure? She's awfully late."

"I'm sure. I'll see you in a couple of days." He held her arm for a moment, then looked quickly about the room as she walked away.

Carrying a suitcase in one hand, his briefcase in the other, Michael rode the escalator back to ground level and found an empty telephone booth. He dropped a dime, propped his foot against the folded door, and dialed his number at home. No answer. Where *was* she?

He resumed his position with the baggage and walked to an information desk at the heart of the terminal. A girl behind the counter took Talia's name and had her paged. Michael listened as the message came over the loudspeaker and watched for Talia in the concourse of people.

"Would you try one more time?" he asked.

"Sure, if you want. But they always show by now."

"No, that's okay, thanks. Forget it."

The inside of the cab smelled heavily of cologne. It was a scent which Michael, for no real reason, seemed to associate with Talia. It came to him suddenly, sitting in the cab in this *déjà vu* of smell, that Talia never wore perfumes anymore. When had she stopped? He couldn't remember; except for the faintest memory of her saying something about her senses becoming too acute. There were other things, changes; most had been gradual, subtle—or was it that he had been too busy to notice? And now, her not being at the airport to pick him up. It was totally out of character for Talia to be late. There had to have been an accident—she wouldn't forget him this way! She was uncomfortable in traffic, he knew; always a nervous driver. He watched both directions of traffic on the expressway, craning his neck to see the far lanes, searching for her tan Audi among the passing and oncoming cars.

He had yelled at her yesterday, and now, something had happened, he knew it. Something was wrong. Talia could be dead.

The garage door opened; a gaping, cavernous mouth.

Talia pulled in, then pressed the control to lower the mechanical jaw. After turning off the ignition to the Audi, she picked up a stack of books from the back seat and walked into the house.

The electric clock over the kitchen sink made a grinding, deafening noise. Like everything now, it was a racking irritation which screamed inside her brain. She held a cloth under a stream of water, than ran it over the cabinet top trying to rub away the cheap gold stars on the slick tile surface. She rinsed the dishcloth and wiped the tops and sides of each canister and then returned each one to its place. Sliding her cookbooks forward, she aligned all the spines so the books made a long, even row. At the stove she wiped the damp cloth around the aluminum rim of a burner; then a second; and a third. As she started on the fourth, she heard a sound at the front door. She stopped, abruptly, listening for the bell. Instead, the door opened and she heard a loud thump on the floor.

"Talia?" It was Michael!

She tossed the dishcloth into the sink and ran to the front of the house.

"Where the hell were you?" he said when he saw her. "Are you all right?"

It was as if she were a child and had erred; she couldn't speak.

"Why weren't you at the airport? I called home—where the hell've you been?"

"I forgot." Her words cracked like brittle.

"How could you forget? I talked to you yesterday!"

Was it yesterday?

"How did you get home?" She followed him upstairs, carrying his attaché case.

"How do you think I got home? A cab. I waited nearly an hour!" He threw his bags on the bed. "I thought you must have had a wreck, that something had happened."

"I'm sorry," she said, easing the case to the floor.

He snatched his tie from his collar. "Forget it."

"I was at the library. I guess I got so involved—"

"Look, I said it was okay."

"But it isn't. It's unthinkable that I could do such a thing."

"You're human."

"Am I?" It startled her. "I never seem to do anything right, anymore."

"It isn't that big a deal. Let's just let it drop."

"You had to take a taxi. It must have cost at least fifteen dollars."

"I'm not worried about the money, Talia."

"Michael, I completely forgot you."

"Look—" he took her hands. "This hasn't been an especially pleasant homecoming so far. Let's see if we can improve things."

"How?"

"For one thing, promise me you'll go to the doctor."

"*Michael.*" She emphasized his name as a plea.

"That's all I ask. Do it and get Joan off my back."

"I wish she'd leave me alone."

"Go to the doctor and she'll leave us both alone. Is it a deal?"

"There's nothing wrong with me."

"So go to the doctor and settle it. Talia, that's all I ask."

"I dislike doctors." She pulled away from him. "I don't want to go."

"But you will?"

It was happening as it always did: she was being defeated with no place to go but to the conqueror. She said what she had to say: "Yes, I will go."

Michael walked peremptorily from the bathroom, a towel tied at his waist, another used to dry his hair. "What time's your appointment?" he said.

"Eleven." Talia turned from him, his towel spreading open as he sat on the bed.

"I'll drive you to Athens if you want."

"No need."

"You're sure?"

"Michael, it's not like I'm ill. We're going this to placate my mother. Remember?" She removed underwear from a bureau drawer and slipped panties over her feet, her robe still tied about her. She then wrangled with a bra, trying to fasten it, pulling her arms from the wrapper's sleeves.

"This is like seeing Houdini," Michael said, watching.

"Will you be home for dinner?"

"Probably. Make sure you have plenty of gas before leaving town. Write down the mileage."

She pulled on panty hose under her robe.

"And go ahead and write a check for the bill. I don't want to be obliged to one of your father's cronies."

Talia finished dressing in privacy as Michael shaved, his electric razor buzzing from the bathroom, torturing her ears.

"Michael, I'm going," she said as she fastened the top button of her blouse.

"Already?"

"I want to give myself plenty of time."

He came to the door of their bedroom, his mouth full of paste, foaming like canned whipped cream. "You're certain you don't want me to go?"

"I'm certain."

"I hope he doesn't find anything."

"He'll find nothing, Michael. Absolutely nothing."

At a self-service island Talia pumped her own gas. She paid the attendant, then logged the car's mileage and the number of gallons of fuel she had bought.

Pulling the seat belt taut, she adjusted mirrors, then started the engine. She followed Northside Drive to the expressway and drove along Interstate 75 until she came to the perimeter. Highway 285 ran for sixty miles around the city of Atlanta, almost exactly the distance from her house to Athens. She turned the heat off, rolled down the window, removed her gloves, and placed her hands high on the steering wheel. She sat far enough back in the seat so her legs were uncomfortably stretched in order to reach gas pedal and brake. She could withstand the elements: hands could tolerate cold; muscles should be tested.

As Talia coursed the perimeter of Atlanta, she imagined the country as it would be driving to Athens. She would pass Snellville and all the growing little communities which felt a tremor each time Atlanta stretched. She would pass John Deere's and Kubota's; red clay fields; dirty roadside stores. She would pass the barn Mother used to sketch each spring and fall, trying to catch the differing shadows.

When she had circled the entire sixty miles, Talia exited, pulled the Audi into a Shell station, and parked near a beverage stand. She was near Marietta now, not far from where she had started.

With the motor off, Talia held to the steering wheel and watched herself walk to the entrance of Dr. Abelard's office. A bell would sound, as she opened the door, and a blur would show behind the bubbled glass at the reception desk. Talia would press the buzzer and the glass would slide; the blue would become the face of a nurse, her mouth placed on upside down. The woman would look through Talia, as if she were vapor, then read the name Talia would print on the pad.

"Oh! Mrs. Sinclaire's daughter. How are you, dear?" And Talia would take form when identified with Mother.

She would be asked to take a seat: "He's with a patient just now. It'll be only a few, few minutes, Ms. Sinclaire."

"No; my name is Freeman now," but the nurse would ignore this and separate them again with the glass.

Inexpensive upholstery would slide beneath Talia's thighs and she would stare ahead at Currier and Ives on pea-green walls. The matting on the prints would be faded; the glass sinking in ripples; the cheaply made,

slanting frames perpetuating constant straightening.
Minute upon minute would pass as Talia would try un-
successfully to read material from ladies' magazines
and outdated newspapers. And then her name would
be called, and Talia would look up to see a white-clad
figure waiting for her down the hall. Her legs would be
blocks of petrified wood as she struggled with herself to
reach the door.

"Miss Talia, how we've grown. You're practically a
woman." The milky figure would flow through the corridor, leading Talia to a cubicle containing: The Long
Green Table; the Doctor's dark steel Desk; the Glass
Cabinet holding his hideous tools.

"Let's strip all the way this time. Drop our pants.
The doctor will want to get a Pap test." The nurse
would watch as Talia undressed. She would stick a
thermometer in Talia's mouth, check her weight, and
pulse, all swiftly and methodically, then leave the
room.

Talia would be alone; she would sit upon the table,
the stiff tissue crinkling under her weight, a rough,
graying sheet pulled under her arms. Again she would
wait, for hours it would seem; her legs dangling from
the table, her back aching from lack of support, her
nipples cold and unforgivably erect; the odious smells
of ethanol and ether congesting in her brain. And then
she would hear him, his gruff voice speaking her name,
the shuffle of papers outside as he looked through her
file. Then the door would open. The incubus would
emerge, bent, with a simian stride.

"Well, who do we have here?" Her skin would
revolt at his touch. "She's developing into quite a
woman, don't you think?" The nurse would answer
with a licentious smile. "What does your daddy think
about his girl growing into such a woman?" And then
he would lift her legs and pull them around, the table
and her body now parallel. "Okay, Missy, let's get a
look-see."

Malevolent hands would depress her abdomen and
knead her breasts. "Getting a little tummy, aren't you,

Miss," and then they would laugh, he and the nurse, and he would give Talia that lecherous wink.

He would pull her to a sitting position again, and an icy instrument would be mashed against her back. She could smell the fetid odor of cigarettes from his breath as he breathed heavily down her neck.

"Okay, Missy, let's get this done." She would lie back down. The nurse would separate Talia's legs and place her feet in metal stirrups. "Let's scoot down toward the front a bit, Miss." He would pull at her bare bottom until it reached the table's edge and she would feel the heat of the lamp and see the top of his yellowing white hair. She would then look away and study the texture of the ceiling, counting the panels, to palliate the horror of his probing.

"Everything's in order," he would say as he stood from the metal stool, pulling rubber sheaths from his hands. "You're the healthiest of that family, I believe. Someday you'll be dropping them like potatoes in a pot." And he would exit, with the nurse, leaving Talia stretched across the obdurate surface of the examining table, starkly exposed.

Talia started the car, readjusted the mirror, and retraced the route she had taken from home. It was finished now; it was done; she could forget it.

That evening Talia watched as Michael ate crepes, making certain none of the sauce escaped him, that he enjoyed the flavor of mushroom and crab.

"What did the doctor say?" He sipped white wine.

"Exactly what I expected him to say."

"Which was?"

"That I'm fine. Do you want more salad?"

"Tell me exactly what he said."

"I told you, he said I was fine."

"But I want to know what happened. He must have thought something about your weight."

"For the hundredth time—I tell you, my weight is fine—fine, fine, *fine*."

"He said that?"

"Certainly. Do you like the crab?"

"Love it. What else?"

"When I got there he was with another patient. I had to wait about thirty minutes. That's not bad for Abelard; he's usually late. The office was the same as it always has been. All those insipid snow scenes on the wall. He hasn't renovated in fifteen years."

"I don't want a description of his decor. What did he say when he saw you?"

"He called me Missy and said I was developing into quite a woman." Michael laughed softly at this.

"They took my temperature, checked my pulse, my weight, examined me and gave me a Pap smear. Afterward he said everything was in order. He said what he always says, that I'm the healthiest of the lot."

"And that was it?"

"Yes; unless you want all the gory details."

"He didn't say anything about your weight?"

"I *told you,* my weight is fine. Perfectly normal; perfectly healthy. He even said I was getting a tummy."

"Did you call your mother?"

"Not yet."

"*Do.* The sooner the better. Maybe now she'll leave me alone."

"She didn't go to the doctor," Dr. Sinclaire's voice whistled on the line.

"Of course she did," Michael said.

"Not according to Ben Abelard."

"What are you talking about?"

"Joan was concerned when Talia didn't come by the house this afternoon after her appointment. So she phoned Abelard's office and the receptionist said Talia had called and canceled."

"I don't believe that."

"Are you questioning me, young man?"

"Of course not. It's just that—you know Talia— she's incapable of a lie."

" 'Sin has many tools, but a lie is the handle that fits them all.' "

Damn quotes! Michael clinched his teeth to prevent the words from spewing from his mouth.

"We expected you to take care of this matter, Michael."

"I can't believe she would fabricate such a thing," he said. "She simply doesn't do things like that."

"Apparently she's changed."

She wouldn't do that, Michael thought. Talia wouldn't lie.

"*Are* you going to take care of this, Michael?"

"Yes."

"Or do we have to assume responsibility for our daughter ourselves?"

"I *said,* I'll take care of it." He slammed down the phone.

As Michael mixed himself a drink, he mentally went over the things Talia had said. The story was too complete; too thorough. Talia had faults, but the one thing she was, was truthful. Honesty was as firmly embedded in her character as pride was solidified in the matrix of her father.

Michael could hear water from Talia's shower as he mounted the stairs. The door to the bathroom was locked.

"Talia?"

He heard the shower curtain being pulled across the rod.

"Yes?"

"Talia, that doctor's office was in Athens; right?"

"Yes." Her voice was strong.

"His name was Dr. Abelard?"

"Yes, Abelard."

Michael felt a chill. "And he said everything was fine?"

"Yes, Michael."

"All right, Talia." And for lack of her, he stroked the wooden door with the palms of both hands.

=7=

Michael watched the straw mat slide against linoleum as Talia pulled her self up and over her knees.

"Eleven . . . twelve . . ." she said vigorously.

She had been performing sit-ups on the kitchen floor since he entered the room. Perspiration stained a much-too-large navy sweat shirt and a faded pair of jeans.

"Fourteen . . . fifteen . . ."

Michael had slept fitfully: Talia had lied. "*Why? Why* would she do it? He had questioned himself through the night as he drifted in and out of sleep. He had stirred restlessly, awakening each time to find Talia out of bed. Once, in darkness, he had heard the soft beat of her running in place followed by the steady swooshing of the exercise bike. And another time he awoke to find her studying under the dim light of her desk downstairs.

"Eighteen . . . nineteen . . . twenty . . ." She had not slowed since he entered the kitchen.

"Good morning, Talia."

She kept perfect time as she replied. "Twenty-one—you're late for your breakfast—twenty-two . . ."

"Talia, it's cold in here. Why haven't you turned up the heat?"

"Twenty-four . . . twenty—"

"Talia, do you always stay awake at night? I mean, *all* night?"

She responded with a loud exhale as she rolled over unbending knees.

68

"I heard you exercising at three in the morning. And later there was a light on downstairs."

"I was studying."

"How long have you been doing this?"

"Twenty-seven . . ."

"Talia, *why* do you stay awake all night?"

"I can't sleep."

"Why?"

"It's a waste, Michael. Sleep is a luxury I can't afford. Twenty-nine . . . thirty . . . thirty-one . . ."

Michael took a seat at the kitchen table, observing from overhead as Talia metronomically pulled up and bent forward, touching head to knees, fingertips to toes.

He searched her face. It had changed. She had never been the kind of beauty that, say, Carolyn was—the kind a man wanted immediately to embrace. But Talia had been beautiful in her own austere way. She had once seemed untouchable to Michael with those perfectly chiseled features, smooth alabaster skin, dark ethereal eyes. Her neck had been long and elegant, accentuated by the style and color of her hair; it had been cropped short, as if a bowl had been placed over her head and shears had followed the outline around; and it was such a deep, shining black that it had, at times, appeared almost blue. She had seemed as rare and as fragile to him as the porcelain figures the Sinclaires displayed on their library shelves, protected beneath glass domes.

But she wasn't the same. Not really. The angular profile he had always admired (it had lent an air of the aristocratic) had now become jaundiced, even flaccid. And she had become so frugal as to avoid having her hair trimmed. It had grown unevenly over the last few months and now hung limp, lusterless, around her neck.

"Forty-eight . . . forty-nine . . . fifty." Talia stood from the mat and, bending at the waist, bobbed up and down touching her toes fifteen or twenty times. She then stood erect, raised her arms overhead and stretched.

"You're exercising a great deal these days, aren't you?" Michael said.

She rolled the mat, patting it at the ends to keep it even, then tied it with a string she pulled from a pocket in her jeans. That was Talia, Michael thought as he watched her: neat, compact, efficient.

"Aren't you going to be late, Michael?" she said to him. "You're always gone by now."

"I thought we might have breakfast together today."

"No!" She stared at him. "No, go ahead. Yours will be cold."

"Talia, when *do* you sleep?"

"I told you I have not the time. My body does not require it." She took a pencil from a drawer and made a check mark on a large cardboard poster tacked to a cork bulletin board. The chart was divided into squares; the days of the week running down the left side, names of exercises printed across the top. The record showed she had progressed steadily, sometimes doubling or even tripling the number of exercises she had completed the day before. She was now at the rate of fifty sit-ups, twenty-five push-ups, hundreds of toe-touches and bends.

"You've improved, haven't you?" Michael said.

Talia looked at the chart. "Especially with running."

"When do you do that?"

"In the afternoons, after my last class."

"How far do you go?"

"I run three miles or walk six."

"Talia—*three miles?*"

"Yes." She was beaming.

"Don't you think you're overdoing?"

"Michael, why must you always let your food get cold? I'll have to heat it again."

"Talia, I think you can do too much too soon."

"I'm the picture of health."

"That's what Dr. Abelard said?"

She turned from Michael and began arranging placemat and napkin on the table, then china and flatware. She took meticulous care in making sure the utensils were equidistant from the plate and the dish was evenly centered on the mat.

"Talia, how much do you weigh?"

"Do you want coffee?" She placed a cup and saucer on the table and poured herself hot tea from a small blue pot, filling her cup only halfway.

"Talia, I asked you a question."

"Did you know that black coffee has more calories than plain tea?"

"No, I didn't know."

"Tea has one calorie, whereas coffee may have as many as four."

She brought a single boiled egg from the stove and laid it upon her plate as if she placed a sacramental offering upon an altar. She pulled her chair away from the table and stood. Carefully, she secured her napkin under the neck of her sweat shirt so it hung at her chin. With the handle of a knife she slowly tapped along the equator of the egg until the shell was shattered.

"Do you know what an eggshell fracture is, Michael? Allyson incurred one when she was eight months old. She fell from the crib during the night when awakened by the phone. A prank call."

"Talia, is that all you're going to eat?"

"An eggshell fracture is different from a depressed fracture in which a fragment is depressed below the surface and may push on the brain. James told me that. He would have made a brilliant surgeon, don't you think?"

"How about some toast or bacon?" Michael transferred a piece of bread from his plate to hers.

"Don't do that!" She returned the buttered toast, wiped her plate with the napkin, and washed her hands before returning to her task. She peeled the egg, gradually, concentrating fully on the act, gently placing bits of shell in a neat pile on the plate.

"Why don't you sit down, Talia?"

"We used to put eggshells in the bird cage. Did I ever tell you we had a bird? A parakeet? James named him." Her face went solemn. "I fear Father was offended we didn't name him something dignified. Like Socrates or Hegel. Or Bacon?" she said gravely. "Bacon laying eggs."

"How long does it take you to peel an egg, Talia?"

"The bird died."

"If this is all you have for breakfast, what do you eat for lunch?"

"How could I possibly eat lunch? After all this."

"Talia, I'm serious."

"So am I." She turned the handle of a pepper mill over her plate until the peeled ovum was more black than white. She stared at the egg for some moments, with a knife in her hand, then suddenly turned to him. "Aren't you going, Michael? You'll be late."

He stood from the table and pulled on his suit coat. "I noticed all those cookbooks you borrowed from the library are due." She was glaring at the food again. "Talia, did you hear what I said about the books?"

"I'll return them."

"You also need to make sure the Christmas cards are sent. Have you done that yet?" She made a small incision with the knife. "Talia!"

She stared at him. "I heard you." She returned to the egg. "Do the yellows ever remind you of eyes?"

"And Talia, you need to purchase gifts for the men at the office. I've already given you the list. Can you take care of it?"

"Piscine eyes."

"Talia, will you take care of the gifts?"

She nodded.

"Be ready to go when I get home tonight. That dinner party starts at six."

She pulled the transparent membrane from the inside of the halved egg white, now free of its yolk.

"Talia, you won't forget the party?"

"No."

She was cutting the white into cubes as he walked to the door. He put his hand on the knob and stopped.

"Talia—I know you didn't see Dr. Abelard yesterday." She remained silent, her back to Michael. "Talia," he said gently, "why did you lie?"

"I had to."

"I don't understand."

"You made me. You forced me to lie."

"How can you say that?"

"There was no *need* for me to see that man. You wouldn't listen to reason. You insisted. I had to lie. You made me."

She held the knife in midair, her eyes again on the table. "I had to, Michael. Can't you see?"

Carolyn stood at her apartment door, dressed for work, a glass of juice in her hand.

"Can you spare a cup of coffee?" Michael walked inside.

"Sure, if you don't mind instant."

"That's great."

"What's up? I thought you were usually at the office long before now."

He followed her to the kitchen. "I missed you."

"Yeah?" She turned and kissed him, tasting of orange. "I'm flattered. But I also have the sneaking suspicion something's wrong. You don't look right."

"Just tired, I guess."

He watched as she put a kettle of water on the stove. He followed the movements of her body, the way her skirt fit smoothly over her perfect behind. Carolyn was slim; the way he liked women. But she was also padded enough to show curves; to still be soft to the touch.

"Carolyn, how much do you weigh?"

"Good grief, I don't know. Around a hundred fifteen, I suppose."

"Do you ever diet?"

"Do I need to?"

"No."

"Then why are you asking me this?"

He said: "I'm totally fascinated by your body," and nibbled on her ear.

She poured steaming water over the instant coffee and stirred in the two teaspoons of sugar he required. "How's work?" she said, offering him the cup.

"Okay."

"It sounds like the Miami-to-London might not go through after all."

He nodded.

"I imagine Frank is clawing the walls."

"Probably."

He removed a novel from the table and absently looked at the cover.

"Have you read it?" she said.

He shook his head.

"They're calling it his triumph. Borrow it if you like."

He loved her when she was this way: energetic, talkative. He wanted to join her, pull himself to her level, but was unable. Instead he let himself be eased by the softness of her presence, drifting among the highs and lows of her voice.

"I finished it last night—Mike, are you listening to me?"

"I'm sorry. What were you saying?"

"Something's bothering you."

"Ah, the psychiatrist. Always at work."

"You're never like this. What's wrong?"

"I didn't sleep well."

"I've never known a lack of sleep to slow you."

He laughed, enjoying the intimacy of her remark. "Yeah, well, I guess I've had less than usual lately."

"Do you want to talk?"

"You don't want to hear my problems, Doctor."

"I'm suddenly altruistic. Besides, you look pitiful."

"It'll probably sound stupid."

"Try me."

"Talia lied. You see—" he tried to explain, "she

never lies. She's incapable of it. She's absolutely the most honest person I've ever known."

"No one is incapable of a lie."

"But this wasn't a little white one. It was an elaborate, premeditated fabrication. She was scheduled to go to the doctor, but instead she canceled the appointment, and when I got home last night she acted as if she had gone. She went into great detail about what the doctor did and said."

"Why was she going to a doctor in the first place?"

"Her mother wanted it. She thinks Talia needs a checkup."

"Well, it's obvious she didn't want her mother telling her what to do."

"There's more to it than that. She said I made her lie. That I forced her into it."

Carolyn clapped her hands and laughed: "That's great! I love it."

"I don't think it's funny."

"Well, she's right, actually; at least in her mind. She was being forced to do something she couldn't accept and therefore she lied."

"Another thing—she's too skinny."

"Why don't you leave the girl alone?" Carolyn stirred her coffee with determination. "The latest surveys show the single woman is happier than the married. Good Lord, I believe it."

"What do you mean by that?"

"Listen to yourself! She's a grown woman. If she wants to be skinny, let her be skinny, for Christ's sake."

"You think I'm making too much of it?"

"I do."

"Maybe you're right."

"I am right." She walked to him, her arms going around his neck. "Do I get to see you tonight?"

"I wish. I have a dinner party to attend. Business; I can't miss it."

"I'll live," she said, and trailed behind him, her arms now at his waist as he walked to the door.

• • •

"Right away?" Michael said.

"Yes." His secretary handed him a folder. "Mr. Rhoades said to have you come to his office as soon as you got in."

"Christ! The one day I'm late and the president of the company wants to see me. Did he say what he wants?"

"No, sir. Do you want coffee?"

"Call his secretary and tell her I'm on my way."

"Yes, sir."

Michael gathered files from several recent projects and slipped them into a leather folder, preparing for anything the old man might want to discuss. He went to the men's room, checked his tie and hair. He always dreaded a confrontation with Rhoades. He was the kind of man who, without asking a question, could make a person reveal everything. Michael took the elevator to the eighth floor, then went to the bathroom again. When he returned to the hall he stood for a moment, composed himself, then turned the handle of the door.

The reception room was plush. Michael walked to the secretary, an attractive woman in her late thirties, impeccably dressed.

"Go right in, Mr. Freeman. Mr. Rhoades is expecting you." Michael smiled, pleased she knew his name, and searched her face for any significance to the meeting.

"Come in, Michael." The man stood behind an enormous desk, free of paper and clutter. He extended a soft, liver-spotted hand, incised at the wrist by a stiff white cuff. "May I have Peg bring you coffee?" The collar of his oxford shirt cut into his cultivated chin as he sat.

Michael said: "No, thank you, sir. I'm fine." His throat felt swaddled; dry.

The man hesitated for a moment, studying Michael's face. "We take great pride in the people we choose to represent Coastal Airlines." Rhodes stopped again as he snipped the end of a cigar. Michael felt obliged to give some response.

"Yes, sir."

"Smoke?" He was offered the cigar.

"No. Thank you." He wished he did.

"Michael, there is no area in this company more important than our legal branch and the reputation that department upholds. Frank Stoner has been chief counsel to this airline for a very long time. He's done some good things." Rhoades drew on the cigar. "But Frank Stoner is no longer the kind of representative Coastal likes to show to the outside world. Do you understand?"

It was happening! "I think so."

"Michael?" He hesitated again. "Michael, there are going to be changes made and we have our eyes on you. You're going to transcend. The sooner the better."

"Thank you, Mr. Rhoades." He avoided a smile and kept his hands together on his lap.

"We need more young men like you. Hardworking, moral, family men."

"I appreciate that, sir."

"You keep things moving as they have been, son. You're doing exactly as you should. And make sure everything is solidified at home. There are no problems there, correct, Michael?"

"No, sir. Everything is fine."

"Good. Keep them that way." He stopped and studied Michael, expressionless.

"Yes, sir. I will."

"I hope we'll see you and your wife at the get-together tonight. I look forward to meeting her."

"Yes, sir. We'll be there."

"Excellent." He took Michael's arm and ushered him to the door. "We'll be talking again."

They were seeing Frank Stoner as Michael had hoped. It was all a matter of time and he would be sitting at Frank's desk.

"Okay, Sue, you can bring me that coffee now," he spoke as he stepped from the elevator.

"You have company, Mr. Freeman," the secretary warned as Michael opened the door to his office.

Frank Stoner sat at Michael's desk, drinking from Michael's initialed cup.

"There's my Boy Scout! Having a good morning, Freeman?"

"What can I do for you, Frank?"

"Coffee was all I could get out of that girl of yours. I'm sure you have something else hidden around here, don't you?"

"What do you need, Frank?"

"Those reports I asked for yesterday." He made no attempt to move from Michael's chair.

"Sue's typing the last one now."

"You're slow, Mike boy. I'm glad it wasn't anything pressing."

"I'll have it for you in half an hour."

"I hear you've been up to Grandpa Rhoades's office for a little chitchat."

"News travels fast."

"To me it does." Frank recrossed his legs on top of the desk. "What'd he do? Fill you with a chest full of hope, Freeman?"

"Like you said, Frank, it was a chat."

"Did he offer you a cigar and pat you on the back?"

"Frank, I have work. Do you mind?"

Stoner's expression changed as he stood. "Just you be careful, Michael. I am not to be counted out. Not yet!"

=== 8 ===

Michael jogged over his front walk and leaped up the steps to his house.

This was going to be a good evening; an excellent evening. He would take Talia to the dinner party and then out afterward, if she wanted, for drinks.

He had thought of her all afternoon, remembering when they met. She had been merely a child. It was when he and her brother James were in college together at the university in Athens. She was much younger than they, still in junior high school at the time. But even at that age she was more sincere than most of the girls in college and more intellectual than most adults. It had not been until after her brother's death, when she was finally older, that Michael had summoned enough nerve to treat Talia as an adult and ask her out. He had spoken to her briefly at James's funeral, feeling he shouldn't stay too long. But Talia had seemed less grieved than alone; he had sensed that she wanted him to stay, that talking with him made James's absence less painful. He called a few weeks later and she had said in that small, sharp voice of hers that yes, she would very much like to see him. He saw her every weekend after that, always driving to Athens and usually staying at the Sinclaire home for one or two days. There had been that period of proving himself, of living up to some tacit kind of test he felt the Sinclaires put him to. He had been working for a tiny law firm in Decatur at the time and when he landed the job with the airlines he felt that at last he had risen; that he had "passed" their test and Talia was his prize.

But it seemed now he never had made the mark. The new job, the money, the house; none of it meant success in the Sinclaires' eyes. And almost from the beginning of their marriage Talia had seemed different from the way he had thought she would be, different from the way she was on those weekend stays at her parents' home. But then, possibly, he was different too. He wasn't the patient, pipe-smoking, benevolent kind of consort he had imagined himself to be. He had made mistakes in their brief marriage; he admitted it. He could be too harsh, too uncompromising. But he would try, honestly try, to make things better, to show Talia how much he loved her, how much he had always loved her, starting tonight.

"Talia? Hey, I'm home. You ready?" He dropped his briefcase near the door. The latch broke with the blow and the contents of the case fell out, forming a portent on the floor. "Ah, damn!" he said and stuffed the papers back inside. He called upstairs again: "Hey, Talia! Are we ready to go?"

"Go where?" She came from the kitchen dressed in the same grimy sweat shirt and jeans she had worn at breakfast. Her hair was damp and stuck to her brow; a fine line of perspiration had formed and lay across her thin upper lip.

"Why are you dressed that way?" He panicked, his voice too loud.

"I've been running."

"Talia, we're supposed to be at the party by six!"

"I went three and a half miles today, Michael. The first of the week I'll be up to four."

"Talia, it's almost five thirty." He felt as if his throat were being constricted by a metal band.

"I ran at the Northside track. It's a good surface but I don't like the crowd."

"Talia, I specifically told you to be ready when I got home. This is an important engagement."

"What engagement?"

"Oh, hell!"

"Michael, please do not swear."

"Talia, there are things happening in my life. I need cooperation. A little support. Every time I feel I'm standing solid, the earth sinks underneath me."

"I could get ready," she offered.

"Look at you. It would take an hour to shower and dress."

"I'm sorry, Michael. Truly."

"You always are," he said, picking up his coat.

"You're going?"

"Of course I'm going. I'll tell them you're sick."

"I'm not!" she said fiercely.

"What would you have me say? My wife doesn't give a horse's rear end about my career?"

"Crude!" she said and turned. He followed her to the kitchen.

"I don't have time to discuss this with you now. But Talia, there are going to be changes made. There's—" he stopped, his eyes on the kitchen table. "What the hell is this?"

The table was loaded with grocery store hams and cellophaned packages of cheese. She ran a hand over one of the large shoulders of meat and said: "They're the Christmas gifts. I did what you wanted. I purchased them today."

"You bought Winn Dixie hams and blocks of goddamn cheddar cheese for the president of Coastal Airlines? Talia, these aren't migrant workers."

"It's good food."

"It's care package material!"

"I spent a great deal of money."

She stood rigid, arms stiff at her sides.

"Well, don't worry yourself about it, Talia. I'll take care of this and everything else. I guess I thought I could count on you for once. But you fooled me again, didn't you?"

"Michael? Please? I don't want you to go."

He slammed the back door as he left the house and ran the Porsche over the curb as he pulled out of the drive. He had planned to tell her about the news at work; about the meeting with Rhoades. To hell with her! He had meant to shower and shave before going to the party. To hell with that too. He could do it all someplace else.

Arms wrapped tightly about her ribs, Talia held herself.

I guess I thought I could count on you for once. Michael's accusation echoed around the room; the clock over the sink ticked rhythmic allegation. She *had* handled it, hadn't she? The gifts were wonderful; she caressed one of the hams.

And why should Michael insist she go? She detested smoke-filled rooms and trivial conversation. If he must go—let him! She imagined him now, a drink in hand, explaining her absence to his associates. Michael needed her at a time such as this. There was satisfaction in the thought.

The box of laxatives rattled empty. Talia threw it into the wastebasket and opened a new box of purgatives, removing two pills. Was she truly a bad wife? Maybe she was not all she should be? She took the medicine, drinking little water. She swallowed over and over, dryly, trying to dislodge the protrusion in her throat. It was a comfort in its pain.

Talia glared at the bounty of food on the table.

Talia, these aren't migrant workers.

It's good food.

It's care package material!

"I spent a great deal of money!" she said aloud and tore the wrapper from one of the hams. Juice ran onto the table as the meat was unclothed.

Talia pulled a large Swedish knife from a magnetized rack. With one full swift blow she cut deeply into the ham. She swung again, this time slicing the viand in half. Two more strokes and it was quartered. The scent of smoked flesh covered her hands.

Pork was fed into the gaping mouth of a food grinder; Talia caught the pulverized results in a ceramic bowl. The process was repeated with another ham; then another. She worked quickly, following the directions on a five-by-seven recipe card. Each ingredient was added until she made a smooth, thick paste of the pork. It was then spread copiously over rounded pieces of rye and sourdough bread. She removed thick lips of pimento from a jar and dissected the bright red pepper, using the sections to garnish her creations; each more ingenious, more perfect than the last. Cheese was sliced, and it too was sandwiched and crowned with parsley and olive. Each hors d'oeuvre was then cautiously positioned upon Talia's wedding-present silver and covered with a glistening sheet of foil. There were seven trays in all.

With her shoulder, Talia leaned heavily against her neighbor's doorbell, keeping the trays balanced and in place. There were four children in the Carlyle family; they would have her creativity eaten within the hour.

The father answered the door. Talia did not remember ever knowing his given name; he was an uneducated man; she and Michael did not socialize with the Carlyles. They had been invited over, once, for drinks. Talia had not seen more than five books in the entire house; they had been offered beer for refreshment; the children ran over the Mediterranean furniture (circa 1970); both husband and wife discussed their fruitful construction company on the south side of town. *Nouveau riche,* Talia had decided; she and Michael had never gone back.

"Let me help you, Mrs. Freeman," the man said as he took the trays. His stomach hung over his belt as a melon hangs heavily from the vine. "Come in. Come in. This is a pleasant surprise."

"No, I can't; thank you," Talia said, standing back. "I made canapés for you and the children."

He stood for a moment, stupidly, staring. His head and hands were too small for the rest of the man. "Uh—let me get Helen," he said.

"No! No, don't bother." Talia couldn't tolerate the woman's tasteless, shrill voice.

"This is—uh—this is awfully kind. Awfully nice, Mrs. Freeman."

"You'll find onion in the ones garnished with pimento."

"You're sure you won't come in?"

"Thank you, no." She hesitated for a moment, thinking her work was too good for the man.

Again: "This is awfully nice, Mrs. Freeman." He still stared. "We'll send one of the boys over with the trays tomorrow."

"No hurry." Talia left him standing at the door and hurried across his lawn to hers. She ran up the bricked drive, strengthening her quadriceps with the pull of the hill. She ran easily, effortlessly. She was in fantastic shape, perfect form. In a day or two she would be running four miles. Then five. Six. She laughed aloud as she thought of Michael and his friends filling themselves with liquor and collation; and imagined the Carlyle children stuffing their shoatish bodies with her hors d'oeuvres as they lay, lethargic swine, before the TV. She was superior; superior to them all.

The list was long (it must be long), full of tasks Talia would perform during the night. She would empty the hamper, spray it with disinfectant, and separate the clothes. The washer would be filled with a small load of whites, mostly Michael's underwear: T-shirts and shorts. While the clothes washed she would clean the kitchen of the litter she had produced while preparing the food. Cabinets would be washed, the sink scrubbed, the old oak table cleaned and oiled. Each room in the house would be dusted, the floors swept, carpets vacuumed. She would have to keep moving; keep going. As always the unseen source would stay at her back, an invisible apparition urging her onward. *Keep going; don't waste*, it would goad her. *Don't tarry. Be strong.* It would meet her in every room. She would feel it in every corner. It would slink behind her in the halls. *Keep going!*

Talia placed a second load of clothes in the washer, transferred clean ones to the dryer, and hurried upstairs. She scrubbed the tub, in the bathroom she and

Michael shared, rinsing shower curtain and ceramic sides by adjusting the nozzle overhead. *Keep going.* The process was repeated until the tub was free of abrasive cleanser; the ceramic shined. The sink and commode were treated in the same manner and the entire room was antiseptically sprayed. She coughed, against her will; the fumes from the disinfectant clogging her lungs. *Keep going. Don't waste.* She closed the door of the bathroom and squirted the full-length mirror with window cleaner, rubbing a towel up and down the surface until it was clear and absent of streak. Standing, she looked at her reflection in the glass and touched her face. She pulled the sweat shirt above her chest (she no longer wore a bra, not even when she jogged), her breasts now fully exposed. She ran a hand over them; good! they were not as noticeably convex. She reached for the snap at the waist of her jeans, about to lower them, when she was stopped. *Keep going!* the source demanded of her. *Don't waste!* She was never free of its hold.

Standing, with clean laundry now spread across her and Michael's bed, Talia performed the task of folding clothes. Michael's T-shirts were pressed against the comforter, front side down, folded toward the center at each sleeve, and then in half lengthwise. Each one was creased exactly the same and placed with care in the top drawer of his bureau. Next the socks. Talia picked up a pair; they were provokingly tied together. She unknotted the socks and placed them together with one neat fold. Michael insisted on tossing them into the hamper this way so they would stay together during the wash. He believed she was incapable of matching them correctly and he feared walking into a business meeting wearing a black sock on one foot, a blue on the other. She untied another pair and doubled it over as she had the first. The next pair was dark blue. The next, black. Talia unknotted both pairs, then placed one black sock over each of the blue. She folded the mismatched pairs and placed them inside Michael's drawer.

Only his shorts remained. Talia picked up a pair of

Michael's briefs, ready to double them at the middle. *Why* did he do this? The underwear was torn at the waist, the elastic pulled from the material. She despised imperfection. If it was no good, throw it away. She started to toss the underwear into the wastebasket, then thought better of the idea.

With three pairs of briefs in her lap, she now sat before her sewing machine, threading the instrument with white polyester. She stitched prudently along the edge, sewing the elastic to the shorts. If Michael took better care of his personal items she would not now be wasting valuable time with such as this. She felt the redness go to her face as she thought of him eating, drinking, oblivious to the things she did for him. She raised the foot of the sewing machine and turned the cloth, still pinned by the needle, ninety degrees to the right. With her foot pressed against the pedal, she firmly sewed shut the fly, and sealed the door of the underwear's crotch.

Talia knelt at the window. Sheets of rain covered the glass.

When she was a child she had knelt in just this manner, waiting for those who had left her to come home; they would drive away for the evening and she, afraid to ask when they were to return, would flee upstairs and start her vigil at her parents' bedroom window. Their smells had lingered in the room: in their closets, on their bed, in Father's pipes, and in Mother's perfume and creams which sat upon her bureau. Surrounded by this, her parents' scented aura, she had waited, a kneeling child, praying it would not happen again as it had happened before. She had been six at the time; Allyson seven. They had had the flu, both of them, only Mother decided Allyson had fully recovered but Talia was not yet well enough to go. So she watched from the window, on the Fourth of July, as the others filled the station wagon with picnic supplies and then backed down the drive. The man had been drinking, she had later learned; he was legally drunk when his car ran off the park road and crashed into the playground slide. Allyson never came home.

Now Talia, the adult, waited not for Father and Mother but for Michael, her old fears returning. Salty puddles of tears spattered on the sill, acerbic as ever.

Through the rain, Talia saw headlights turn into the drive. It was three thirty in the morning. She listened for Michael's key in the door. Lights flooded the hall. From the door of their bedroom, she watched the top of Michael's head bob up and down as he climbed the stairs. She noticed for the first time that he was beginning to gray.

He passed her silently, with a glance in her direction. From the door she watched him remove his shoes as he sat on the bed.

Quietly, she walked across the room. She too removed her shoes, the ones she had jogged in, and sand fell from damp socks as she pulled her feet free of Adidas leather. She turned to face his side of the bed. His back was bent as he untied the silk knot around his neck and unbuckled the belt.

"Did you have a nice time?"

His back remained a wall, separating them. He raised a glass and took a long, loud swallow. Talia could smell alcohol from across the room. She picked up his suit coat from the bed; it carried the scent of cigarette smoke and perfume.

"It's awfully late," she said, as she removed a hanger from his closet.

He slammed his glass against the nightstand and grabbed his jacket and the hanger from her hands.

"Look! You are not to question me. Do you understand?"

Talia stepped backward.

"I advise you to leave me alone, Talia," he said.

She retreated to her side of the room. In her corner, back to Michael and shielded by a long blue robe, she unfastened the snap of her jeans.

Michael snatched the robe from around her shoulders. "And I am sick of you undressing that way! I'm your husband!"

Talia ran to the bathroom, slamming the door, trying frantically to lock it when it was kicked open.

"You are not to close that door on me, Talia! Never again!" His eyes were frightening. He jabbed a finger at her chest: "I am your husband!" He pressed her toward the tub: "And you—are my wife! How long has it been since we acted as husband and wife? Four months? Five months? It's been seven, Talia. Seven goddamn months!" The weight of his body pushed against her. "What is it Talia? Am I not good enough for a Sinclaire? Or maybe you're just plain frigid."

"Stop it!"

"Even your hands are like ice." He held her arms, trapping her between him and the wall. She tried to pull free, only increasing his grip. "This is the *last* time you lock me out!"

She fell against the shower curtain, ripping rubber from plastic hooks. He held her wrists as she straddled the side of the tub, a captured animal.

"Michael, stop it!"

He banged against the commode as he pulled her from the tub. "You won't shut me out this time."

"Michael, *please!*"

He pulled at her clothing. She jerked free but he caught her again as she tried to run; he tore at her jeans, yanking them to her knees.

"Oh, Michael, don't!"

He fell over her, the odor of liquor suffocating as he pressed his mouth over hers, and forced apart her thighs.

Michael's breathing slowed as he lay on his back beside her. He coughed and stirred.

He was above her now. His face was pale, his mouth open as he slowly scanned the length of her unfamiliar body, staring at her legs, her stomach, her breasts. He despised the way she looked, Talia thought; she saw it in his eyes.

"Talia—" but his sentence broke as she rolled to her side, pulling up by the commode, protecting herself from his stare.

At last he left her, leaving her huddled on the cold, ceramic tile floor.

=== 9 ===

Talia sat at attention, her palms pressed flatly against the sides of the upholstered seat in Michael's car. Her hands slid stiffly down until her left ring finger touched a sticky blister on the leatherette. The yams. It seemed years now since she spilled the sugary potatoes over Michael's seat. And, paradoxically, what occurred five or ten years ago now seemed to have happened last week. Time filtered in and out of her brain as water flows through the filaments of a sponge; she knew not one tide from another. Yesterday was today, today yesterday, and last month next year.

She removed a folded tissue from the purse on her lap, dampened the paper with her tongue, and rubbed covertly at the syrupy bubble as she stared straight ahead. The streetlights formed chiaroscuro figures on the car's windshield; transient invaders of the night.

"What are you doing?" Without turning she knew Michael watched as she rubbed.

"There was something on the seat," she said. The tissue fell in shreds.

He returned his attention to the road. The street was still wet; it had rained all day, the earth seasoned with a cold, clear broth of precipitation.

Michael's feet changed position on the floor and his hand quickly shifted gears. The car slowed as it neared the amber light hanging over the cross in the road. They slid to a halt and Talia felt his eyes upon her again; hers remained on his braking and clutching feet.

"I wish you would say something," he said.

"I already have. I don't want to go."

"At one time you enjoyed parties. Please, Talia, *try* to have a good time?" His last sentence rose on the word "time," sounding a question as his left foot relieved the clutch and the Porsche lurched forward.

Unanswering, Talia surveyed buildings, houses, trees, lawns, expecting them to weaken with the implication of this night. New Year's Eve. The old year was dying, the new about to be born. She still half-believed a childhood assumption that everything, like the old man costumed as the fading year, died at the stroke of midnight and was born again at dawn on the new year's first day.

"You look nice, Talia. I'm glad you wore the dress."

She turned to him. His head pivoted ninety degrees to face her, then ninety degrees back to view the road. He repeated the process over and over, reminding Talia of a figure which emerges from a Swiss clock and has the functions to move in only such a way. He made the movement again.

"It really looks good, Talia." He emphasized the "good."

Michael had purchased the dress last week. No, last week was Christmas. It must have been two weeks ago; she couldn't remember the day. He had come home from work elated, ushering her to the car—the engine still running—explaining he was going to buy her the most expensive dress in town. She had refused at first, dragging behind him as he pulled her down the drive. But he had insisted and won. She had not wanted to shop; she hated trying on clothes, selecting, paying the price. But again, Michael had insisted, choosing the dresses she was to try and then finally choosing the one she wore tonight.

"You'll have a good time," he was saying to her now. "Just be yourself." What was herself? She started to ask but was afraid he might not know.

"I don't know anyone who'll be there."

"Sure you do. You know Janus and Paul, and all the people who were at our Thanksgiving party. You'll be fine." His voice was not reassuring.

"I don't care for those people."

"Talia, *please*. This is a party given by the president of Coastal Airlines. Can't you understand the importance of that? The members of the board will be there. The president. His wife. Everyone. They'll be watching me."

"You, not me. I don't want to go."

"The impression you make is as important as the one I make. Talia, this one night please try?"

She leaned against the window to her right and studied the landscape. The trees were beginning to die. Their leafless branches extended as pleading hands, struggling to survive the old year's plight.

"You don't have to initiate conversation, but be cordial for heaven's sake. Listen and smile. And carry a drink around with you. Ask for Scotch." He had given her instructions like this since he purchased the dress. "Laugh at their jokes." "Sip on a drink." "Smile."

His eyes were on her again. "Do you feel okay?"

She ignored him and returned her attention to the tacky little glob of syrup on the seat. She scraped at it with her thumbnail, her eyes straight ahead on the road.

"Who do you know at Cross Creek Apartments?" Talia asked.

"Excuse me?" said Michael.

"Who lives at Cross Creek?" He wasn't looking at her now. "I saw our neighbor at the grocery store this morning. She said how strange it was to run into me since she rarely sees either of us and she had just seen you. She said she was leaving Cross Creek Apartments and saw you drive through the gate. She said she blew."

"I didn't see her."

Talia waited as he maneuvered the car around a winding ramp and eased into expressway traffic. She started again: "Who lives there?"

"Oh, at Cross Creek? A corporate doctor doing market research for Coastal. I took some papers by."

"On New Year's Eve?"

"Yes, on New Year's. I needed it done." His voice changed; softer he said: "I suppose school starts again soon?"

She nodded.

"You'll be glad to get back, I imagine."

"Is he single?"

"Who?"

"The doctor. At Cross Creek."

"Uh, yes—single. I was asking you about school." He turned to her again. "What day do you start?"

"I don't know."

"Don't you think you should find out?"

"I'm not going back." She watched the fleeting lights of houses, the passing of cars.

"What do you mean, you're not going back?"

"Exactly what I said; I'm not."

"What about your master's? Your doctorate?"

"I can't now."

"I'm not following you, Talia."

"My grades," she said.

Grades: the mark of one's ability; the display of progress, knowledge, strength. Grades. It occurred to her now she had awaited them all her life. They had marked the apogee and perigee of her existence. The mark of her ability, producing a display or denial of Father's and Mother's Approval and Love.

"What happened?" Michael said.

"In Chaucer; I made a B." With hands pressed tightly to the seat Talia told Michael how she had gone to Emory, the last day of exams, to pick up her grades. Two of her instructors had taped to the doors of their classrooms the usual computer printouts containing student identification, course description, and each student's grade: "English 631—Non-Dramatic Literature of the Sixteenth Century, English Prose and Verse from Skelton to Donne—A"; "English 648—Modern English, Phonology and Morphology—A." The third printout, Chaucer, English 611, had not been taped to the classroom door.

When Talia had knocked at the professor's office he had invited her in. He had bent over his desk; a young, devoted Canterburian who viewed the world from behind quarter-inch-thick wire rims and wiry brown hair that cumulated about his face like a thick, full cloud. "Yes, I have it," he had said. "You made a B for the quarter. I was disappointed with your essay on *Troilus and Criseyde*. You didn't know it well, did you?" He was going over her incorrect analysis of *The Book of the Duchess* when she walked out.

"It can't be as terrible as you make it, Talia."

"I made a B, Michael. In Chaucer."

"It's not the end of the world. Good grief, Talia, most people are thrilled with a B."

"I'm not most people!" And then: "I'm not going back."

"Because you made one lousy B? That's stupid. It makes you human."

"Imperfection? Inadequacy makes one human?" she shrilled.

"God, I'm sorry I brought this up. Calm down, will you."

"I cannot go back to school."

"Okay, Talia, fine. Get a job."

"A job?" She clutched the seat.

"That's what people normally do when they stop going to school."

"What kind of job?"

"We'll talk about it later." He stopped the car. "Now, Talia, don't stand in a corner all night. Be friendly."

"What kind of job, Michael?"

"Put on your coat."

"What *kind* of job?"

"Hell, Talia, I don't know. Be a secretary."

"Father would be furious."

"What do you think he'll be when he finds out you're not going back to school?"

"It must be something special. I'm supposed to have a career."

"We'll discuss it later, Talia. Put on your coat and get out of the car."

All the old pressures had returned, engulfing her. "It must be special, Michael, it *must*."

"All right, Talia, all right. Get out of the car."

And as she did, she felt swallowed by the night.

"Move, Talia," Michael whispered as he nudged her spine with his empty plate.

She turned to him. "You didn't tell me there would be dinner," she said.

"Put something on your plate," he said, his whisper a command. They moved along the buffet.

A Coastal executive and his wife moved along with them on the opposite side of the table. "Well, Talia," the man said, dipping his Saint Laurent sleeve in asparagus as he served himself generous portions of beef. "I understand you're soon to finish your master's."

Michael watched, the muscles of his stomach tensing, as the man waited for Talia's reply. She secured a small piece of meat with a silver tong, examined it, then returned it to the tray and pulled through the slices of beef for another.

"Talia?"

She looked from the food to Michael.

"Stop admiring the food for a minute, honey." He laughed and winked at the man. "You've been asked a question."

"I hear you almost have your master's," the man said again.

"No, I—" she stopped and looked to Michael. "Not as soon as I would like."

"Too impatient," Michael had to take over. "She wants to be finished right away."

"The time seems important now," the man said to Talia. "But it won't in the future; not in ten or twenty years."

"Nothing is frivolous to me, especially time. Your elbow's in the asparagus," she said.

The man checked his sleeve.

"You went to Duke, didn't you?" Michael said, to distract, watching Talia as she toyed with the beef and tongs.

"Duke University. Class of fifty-five. You stick with it, Talia, it won't take long."

"My son's at Duke," someone from behind interjected.

Michael took the opportunity to bend close to Talia. "People are waiting." With a serving fork he placed a large slice of roast on her plate. She stared at him, briefly, then returned the beef to the tray.

The executive's wife had moved forward and was now aligned with Talia.

"How in the world do you stay so thin?" the woman said to Talia, heaping wild rice onto her plate.

"Quite simply," Talia said flatly, moving from the meat. "I imagine there are slugs crawling through my food, eliminating on everything I am to eat."

The woman stared, her plate held at a precarious slant.

Michael laughed too hysterically and put a hand on Talia's arm. "Forgive her," he said. "She's been around me too long. It's something of a private joke."

The woman blinked rapidly. "Well, obviously it works. I'm not half as hungry as I was." She walked from the buffet.

Michael pushed behind Talia and placed two dinner rolls and a spoonful of rice on her plate.

"Don't you dare put that back," he demanded.

She looked at him without expression. "Why, no," she said, "I wouldn't think of it."

To Michael's surprise the rest of the evening was going well. Talia had sat between him and Mr. Rhoades during the meal, and unbelievably, she had eaten her dinner and talked in sharp, intelligent quips the old man seemed to enjoy.

"She's going to be an asset to you, Michael," Rhoades was saying to him now that Talia had left the room. "We need more young couples like you and Talia. Hardworking young people with good heads on their shoulders."

"Thank you, Mr. Rhoades." Michael's face ached from the strain of a constant smile.

"I have to have respect for the people I—"

"Is there a doctor in the house?" Frank Stoner stood inside the entrance that led from the huge living room to the wide and regal foyer.

"What is it, Frank?"

"We have a sick lady upstairs. Looks like Mrs. Freeman had too much to drink."

"Talia?" Michael stood from the sofa.

"I unfortunately intruded upon her privacy. Your little lady was upchucking all over the john."

Mr. Rhoades cleared his throat.

"Talia doesn't drink," Michael defended.

"Not well, apparently."

"Frank, she doesn't drink at all. Something else must have made her ill."

Frank put his arm around Mrs. Rhoades. "He certainly didn't mean the food. Your dinner was delicious." He called after Michael: "First door on the right. Top of the stairs."

From the hallway on the second floor Michael could hear laughter below.

"Talia?" He knocked on the bathroom door. "Talia, are you in there?"

There was a rush of water and then the sound of a lock turning. The door opened.

"Talia, what's the matter?"

"Nothing."

"Are you sick?"

"No."

"Frank said you were."

She stood at the sink washing her hands. Her face was white. "He's a disgusting man."

"Talia, *are* you ill?"

"No."

"You've thrown up. I can smell it."

"She has bad taste in furniture, don't you think? Very little art. With her money you would assume——"

"Talia, everyone thinks you're drunk."

"I *am not!*"

"I'm aware of that. If you're sick, tell me."

"I'm fine."

"All right, let's go." He picked up her purse.

"Home?"

"Not by a long shot."

"I want to go home."

"We're going to walk downstairs and try to salvage this evening while we can."

She sat on the commode seat, face in her hands. Michael wet a washcloth and handed it to her.

"Here, wash your face. Do you have makeup? You look pale."

She shook her head.

"Then pinch your cheeks or something. I've got to think of what we can say when we go back down there."

"We could say I've had a virus."

He watched as she rubbed her face with the rough cloth, her cheeks reddening. The dress she wore was not at all the same fit it was two weeks ago; she had lost more weight. And her hair—he had insisted she have it styled for the party tonight—looked unnatural and brittle. But what seemed the strangest of all to Michael was that it was *she* who had thought of their lie.

"All right," he affirmed. "That's what we'll say."

They left shortly after midnight, sooner than most of the other guests.

Mr. Rhoades held Talia's hand as he walked them to their car. "I hope you'll feel better, my dear. Michael, you take care of this young lady."

"Yes, sir. I will."

Michael waved as they pulled away. Talia sat absolutely still, arms folded rigidly across her stomach.

"You threw up on purpose, didn't you, Talia?"

Michael waited. He watched her spine grow more stiff as she sat away from the seat. "That was a stupid thing to do in someone else's house. And of all people to catch you—Frank Stoner! Why would you do such a thing, Talia?"

She was humming now, studiously ignoring him.

He reached out and touched her hands. They were cold despite the car's heater. Cold and clenched.

"Talia, *please*. *What* is wrong with you? Tell me what's wrong."

=== 10 ===

Ah, damn! That's enough!" Carolyn pushed Michael away. "Carolyn, I'm sorry."

"Why be sorry? Our lovemaking hasn't been good for weeks."

"It's Talia. I'm worried about her, Carolyn."

"Then take her to a doctor, damn it."

He followed her from the bedroom. "You could help if you would."

"I am *not* your analyst. Put on some clothes."

"She sewed up the crotch of my briefs."

Carolyn laughed despite herself. "Well, one thing's for sure, her problem and mine are obviously not the same."

"Don't you think there's something sick about a person who would do that?"

She slammed the door to the bar. "Damn it, I'm out of gin!"

"Last night when I got home she was on her exercise bike riding in the dark—not a light in the house. You know what she said when I wanted to turn on a lamp?"

"I have a feeling I'm going to find out."

"She said, 'There's no need for light. My soul knows naught but my eyes see all.' She talks like that all the time."

After a prolonged silence Michael said: "She rode for thirty-eight minutes. Thirty-eight minutes in the dark."

"Mike," Carolyn's voice lifted, "a friend of mine has a condominium at Ponte Vedra. He said I could use it anytime. Why don't we go—get away for a few days? You could swing it, couldn't you?"

"Talia and I went to Ponte Vedra on our honeymoon." He sat on the couch, nude. "We had a pretty good time, but we weren't home a week when she started putting turpentine around the house. A jar in every room."

"Good God, why turpentine?"

"I didn't figure it out until recently. Her mother's an artist, so you see their house always smells of turpentine and oils. She was trying to make our place smell like her mother's.

"She did the same with tobacco, bought two large tins of the brand her father smokes. She got sick that same week. Flu, I think, I can't remember. But that's when she started to diet, when she was sick and lost a little weight."

"Mike, let's go for a drink. I'm out of gin."

"She's thrown away all the snapshots I took of her on our honeymoon," he said distantly. "Said she didn't want to be remembered looking the way she did then. If the photograph was of a scene she wanted to keep, she cut herself out and kept the other half of the picture."

Carolyn moved bottles around under the sink, looking for a remnant. Nothing.

"She said they made her look fat. But even back then she only weighed a hundred and fifteen pounds."

"Damn it, I want something to drink."

"Carolyn, why would a woman's periods stop?"

"Pregnancy."

"She isn't pregnant. For no reason her periods have completely stopped."

"Menstruation doesn't suddenly cease when you're— what is she?—twenty-two, twenty-three?"

"It has in her case. A few nights ago she was complaining of pain in her stomach and I asked if it was that time of the month. She said, 'Don't be silly. I don't have those anymore.' "

"Menstruation is sometimes stopped temporarily in

female athletes, those who do excessive amounts of strenuous exercise, but I tell you, she's probably pregnant."

"No, can't be. There isn't anything between us anymore."

"Really?" Carolyn looked amused.

"Really. Talia doesn't enjoy sex."

"Has it ever occurred to you there could be someone else?"

"Not Talia. She's celibate."

"Bullshit," Carolyn said mildly.

"She says she hasn't had a period in six or seven months."

"Mike, let's get out of here. Go get something to eat."

"Talia never eats."

"Oh, crap! Enough is enough. She's only trying for sympathy. And would you please put on your clothes?"

"All her senses have become extremely acute. I can be in the next room with the door closed, and she knows if I put on cologne. She hears everything I say."

"You aren't listening, Mike. I want to go out."

"I told you about her being in the dark?"

"Yes, you told me."

"I'm not certain if it's because her eyes are so sensitive or if it's an effort to save money. She's frugal to a fault."

"I'm getting dressed." Carolyn moved toward the bedroom.

"She uses tea bags until they're tasteless. Buys linen napkins to save paper and then uses the same napkin for a week. She bathes—*when* she bathes—in a spoonful of water. Cold water."

"The woman's neurotic!" Carolyn threw his clothes on the bed.

"There was a time when she read a minimum of four books a week. You know what our main topic of conversation is now?"

"I'm dying to know."

"Food. It's all she thinks about."

"You've domesticated her, Michael. Sucked out all her creativity. Made her a wife."

"She never leaves the house anymore. She talks to no one."

"The frustrated housewife, I tell you. She's lost all her confidence. I see it in patients every day."

"She could have a career if she wanted. She went to school to avoid that, I think. Now she's quit school. She's afraid. I think she's afraid of everything."

Carolyn found herself staring at him. He nodded slowly, eyebrows arching. "There's something wrong with her, Carolyn. I know it. Things aren't right."

"Do you know what I think?" Carolyn said coldly. "I think you're making a big deal over nothing."

"She looks so—"

"I *know—thin—*you've told me! She's on a diet. She and half the female population of this country. It's part of our culture. Our society urges women to be skinny."

"Carolyn, I'm convinced she's ill. I don't know if it's physical or mental, but Talia's not well."

"Look, I've paper work to do and you're obviously tired. Why don't we call it quits for tonight?"

"Carolyn, I really *need* to talk."

"Well, I'm sorry. I don't."

He continued: "A few days ago I found a notebook in the top drawer of her bureau. It was a day-by-day account of the past four months; a complete record, to the ounce, of what she had consumed each day. She's made a list of the exercises she performs; how many miles she jogs; her daily weight. There's also a record of the number of times during the day, at the exact hour, she defecates."

"How much did it say she weighs?"

"The last entry was seventy-nine pounds."

Carolyn sat on the bed, clothes in hand.

"I found boxes of laxatives in every drawer, hidden in her clothing. I counted over twenty boxes. And there's an empty one in the trash every two or three days."

"Would you like a drink?" Carolyn said. "Some wine?"

"She doesn't drink either. Not even water. And when she does it's from a calibrated measuring cup so she knows precisely how many ounces she's swallowed. It all goes in her notebook. She's obsessed with food. Even to what happens to it after it's eaten. On the inside of our medicine chest she's taped a schematic drawing of the human digestive system."

"People do all sorts of things for attention, Mike. Maybe she—"

"Carolyn, that's not it. I'm positive. It's more like she's trying to punish herself. When she's reading she stands. And, if she does sit down, she sits on the edge of the chair, her back perfectly straight and unsupported. In the kitchen she's removed all the light bulbs except a forty-watt lamp over the sink. When I offered to put in a stronger bulb she refused. She keeps the heat turned off and sometimes when I come home she's so cold her lips are blue. She's created a contest of sorts, with herself, running up and down the stairs to see how quietly she can do it. She does it every day, each time trying to run more softly. Twenty times up—twenty times down. I've tried to get her to stop but she always says she can't. 'I want to sometimes,' she says, 'but I can't.' Carolyn, I'm really frightened."

"Get her to a doctor, Mike."

"She won't go. When I suggest it, she acts crazy. Screaming about how everyone is trying to make her fat. Even her parents have tried to get her to go."

"You're going to have to treat her as if she were a child. *Insist* she go. Pick her up and carry her if you have to."

"She's unbalanced, isn't she?"

"I don't know. But you can't continue worrying like this. If you really want to help her, get her to a doctor and find out if it's physiological. If not, he can refer you to a psychiatrist. But Mike, she obviously needs professional help."

• • •

As soon as Mike was gone Carolyn went to her study in the small second bedroom of her apartment. She removed a heavy black volume from a shelf over her desk and turned the pages of the book.

She read the definition carefully: "A serious and sometimes life-endangering condition leading to extreme loss of weight, physical atrophy, and malaise; caused by an unremitting pursuit of excessive thinness."

With a pencil she marked the most important symptoms:

> . . . interest in food combined with a denial of hunger . . . athleticism and excessive exercising . . . marked obsessionality . . . removal of food through self-induced vomiting, laxatives, and other means . . . cessation of menstruation . . . excessive devotion to schoolwork . . . sleep problems . . . post-pubertal dependence on mother . . . irritability and lack of humor . . . withdrawal . . .

The top of Carolyn's scalp tingled. She placed a piece of paper between the pages and closed the book. She was certain now. Absolutely. Talia was a classic case of anorexia nervosa.

=== 11 ===

Tell me something about yourself, Talia," Dr. Panighetti said, settling into the embrace of his high-backed swivel chair. The springs of the chair squeaked as he leaned against the upholstery. The noise was a cry in Talia's ears; a piercing lamentation.

"Begin where you like," he said.

"There is nothing to tell," Talia's posture was absolute as she sat forward in the overly cushioned seat. Legs stretched in front of her, feet inches from the floor, she contracted the muscles behind her knees by extending and pointing her toes. For several minutes the only sound was the slight pop of her left ankle each time she arched her foot.

"How old are you, Talia?"

"You're aware of my age."

"I would like for you to tell me."

She made no answer and avoided his eyes by staring at the beveled edge of his desk.

"It is important that we talk if I am to help you, Talia."

"I don't need your help."

"Do you know why you're here?"

"Michael."

"Michael made you come?"

"Yes."

"How do you feel about Michael?"

"He's my husband."

"And how is one supposed to feel about one's husband?"

"I love him," Talia said.

"Do you resent him?"

I resent you, she thought and avoided his query while studying the white ribbon of skin on the ring finger of her left hand. Her wedding band no longer fit; it had grown too large and easily slid over her knuckle and to the floor.

"You resent Michael for bringing you here, don't you, Talia?"

"No! I don't know."

"Is that why you've stopped eating, Talia? To punish Michael?"

"No."

"How much do you weigh, Talia?"

"I weigh what I should weigh."

"Your medical record says you weigh seventy-six pounds."

"Then why did you ask?"

"Don't you think seventy-six pounds is too low?"

"I do not."

"How tall are you, Talia?"

"You have the report."

"Do you know what the average adult female of your height should weigh, Talia?"

"I am not average."

"Do you consider yourself above average?"

She could feel the weight of his eyes upon her downturned face as she fingered the patch of skin where her ring used to wear. She purposefully looked about the room. Everywhere she turned she could feel his stare following. At last, the silence unbearable, she felt pressured to speak.

"My weight is fine."

Without comment he opened a large folder. From where Talia sat (she had exceptional sight; she could pride herself on that), she could see her name printed across the folder's tab. While he studied the papers she tilted her head slightly so she might see him more clearly. Furrows arched wryly over his eyes and cut deeply into his brow. An unruly display of gray and black hair darted wildly from under his eyeglasses and from the nostrils of his large, bulbous nose. A mustache sprouted beneath, mantling the upper lip, and a wiry beard grew under the lower.

He spoke in an unctuous nasalism, the words sliding into one another, his sentences forming a pontificating drawl: "According to your records from Dr. Lambdin, you're suffering from low blood pressure. Are you taking medication?"

"No."

"He also states you are experiencing amenorrhea. That means you—"

"I'm aware of the definition."

"Then you can tell me how long it's been since you've had a period?"

"No."

"Has it been longer than six months?"

"I don't know."

"You can't remember?"

"I guess not."

"Possibly you don't wish to remember."

She refused to reply.

"Does discussing menstruation embarrass you, Talia?"

She looked beyond him to a garish painting on the wall. It was a scene of a ship at sea, the sky a hideous red.

"Dr. Lambdin prescribed a progesterone derivative for the amenorrhea," he said, as if not to her. "Did you take the tablets, Talia?"

"Yes," she lied. She had flushed the fourth tablet down the commode yesterday. One tablet each day so Michael would believe she did as the doctor had said.

"And you have started menstruating?"

"Yes." She twisted uncomfortably in her chair.

"How do you feel about the bleeding?"

"Nothing."

"It doesn't bother you?"

"No."

"Were you glad when your periods first stopped?"

"I suppose."

"Then you were happy?"

"Wouldn't you be? To be rid of the wretched mess?" She silently cursed herself; she should not have allowed her voice to rise.

"Why does menstruating bother you?"

"It doesn't."

"But you said you were glad when you stopped having your periods."

She alternately pointed the toes of each foot; to the ceiling; the floor.

"Do you want to have children, Talia?"

"It doesn't matter."

"You don't care?"

"I shouldn't."

"You shouldn't have children?"

"No," she said. She wanted to be left alone!

"Why is that, Talia, that you shouldn't have children?"

She continued her pedaling of air. Left. Right. Left.

"Are you afraid to have children, Talia?"

"Children get in the way of a career."

"And you want to have a career?"

"Yes."

"What kind of a career?"

"I don't know."

"Is that why your periods have ceased?" He made a clicking noise at the end of each sentence, a noise produced by inadvertently cupping his tongue against the roof of his mouth. "Because you wouldn't like to have children, Talia, that's why your periods have stopped?"

"No!"

"Tell me about your father, Talia." The clicking was growing louder. It snapped repeatedly in her ears. "Do you love your father?"

"Of course."

"Tell me about him."

She covered her ears.

"You don't like to discuss your father?"

She walked to the opposite side of the room to escape the aggravating snapping of his tongue. A long, narrow sofa was positioned against a far wall. She lowered herself to within inches of sitting and then quickly stood again.

"You may sit on the couch if you wish, Talia."

"No!"

"How do you feel about your father?"

"I love my father."

"Are you ashamed of your love for him, Talia?"

"He's my father!"

"And do you love him as a father?"

"This is a ridiculous subject."

"Does it frighten you to discuss your feelings?"

"I don't have to talk about this."

"Do you have trouble expressing how you feel?"

"I do not feel!" She pushed a fist against her leg.

He leaned forward in his chair, producing the same nettling noise as before: "You may sit, if you wish, Talia."

She remained standing, hand gripping an arm of her chair, watching as he slowly removed a brown cigarette from a pewter container on top of his desk. As he lit the cigarette, she saw he was missing the index finger of his left hand. There was an ugly stub, textured by overlapping skin, where the appendage had been rent and healed. The sight produced an odd sensation along the back of Talia's neck. She moved to the front of her chair and sat.

"Tell me, Talia," he said, then blew smoke from the corner of his mouth. "Do you often dream?"

"Sometimes."

"Last night?" he said.

"I can't remember."

She watched as he scratched roughly at his beard, the butt of his missing finger wiggling tragically like a decapitated little animal.

"Think carefully," he was saying. "Did you dream last night?"

"Yes."

"Tell me about it."

"It doesn't make sense."

He waited until she continued.

"I was dressed to come here," she said. "Only I was at my parents' house instead of at home. I was standing at the top of the stairs and Michael was behind me. When I started to descend Father was there. He was smiling at me. He said for me to hurry, that we should go. When I was almost at the bottom, Mother stepped in front of me, and said that red was not my color. The dress I was wearing was red. She said I should change, red was not my color."

Dr. Panighetti drew on the cigarette.

"That's all," Talia said. "That's all of the dream."

With his persecuted hand he snuffed out the cigarette and then leaned backward.

"Are you envious of your mother, Talia?"

"No!"

"Are you jealous because your mother is married to your father?"

"Of course not. No!"

"What do you think the dream means, Talia?"

"I don't know." He waited. "It means I wore the wrong dress. It means nothing."

"Could it mean your mother stands between you and your father, Talia?"

"I want to go home."

"Why did your periods stop?"

"I told you they just stopped." Fingernails dug into her palms. "I don't like your questions."

"Why have you stopped eating, Talia?"

"I don't need food."

"You don't allow yourself food, do you?"

"No."

"Why, Talia?"

"I don't want to get fat."

"You dislike overweight people?"

"Yes."

"Why?" he said. "What does fat mean, Talia?"

"It's ugly. Uncontrolled."

"Is being pregnant ugly and uncontrolled?"

The wall to Talia's left was covered with hundreds

of books. She began counting all the volumes bound in black.

"Would you like to turn and face me?" he said.

She maintained her position. The black count was now at thirty-two.

"Dr. Lambdin wrote on your medical record that you suffer from constipation. Is that why you don't eat?"

Thirty-seven.

"Tell me what it's like when you eat, Talia."

"Uncomfortable."

"*How* is it uncomfortable?"

"I feel as if I'll explode. My stomach can't hold it anymore."

"You don't want your stomach to be full, do you?"

"No."

"Why is that?"

"It's ugly. I need to be thin."

"And being pregnant is ugly, isn't it, Talia?"

"You have forty-six volumes bound in black on those first four shelves."

"Tell me about your father, Talia."

The doctor walked around his desk and stood near her. He lit another cigarette.

"Is he an affectionate man?"

"He's a father."

"How affectionate should a father be?"

Talia stood now also. She walked to the bookcase and began to align Dr. Panighetti's books.

"Is he more affectionate, say, than your mother?"

"No."

"Less affectionate?"

"No."

"Do you wish he were more affectionate, Talia?"

"He is as he should be!"

"That question angers you; why?"

"I don't want to discuss Father anymore."

"Would you like to discuss your mother?"

"No."

"Do you like your mother?"

"Of course! I love Mother!"

"You're angry now."

"Yes," she said.

"Then you are capable of anger, aren't you?"

"I suppose."

He stood behind his chair, seven and a half fingers curled over the leatherette.

"Tell me about food."

"It makes you fat. People push it on you. People want you fat."

"Does Michael?"

"They all do."

"If it makes you fat then food must be evil, isn't that correct?"

"I guess so."

"And that's why you can't eat? Because food is evil?"

"I guess that's right."

"You think the food is evil and it makes you fat."

"Yes."

"Good. Good. We're getting somewhere."

Carolyn thumbed through the folders on her desk, the last of a large stack of paper work that had accumulated over the past few weeks. Her concentration was broken by a buzzer; she picked up the receiver of her phone.

"Yes, Freddie," Carolyn said. "What is it?"

"You have a call; Michael Freeman."

"Fine. Put him on."

"Hi!" She heard Mike's strong, articulated voice on the other end of the line. It had been several days now since they had talked and although she hated admitting it to herself, she had missed him.

"Hi, yourself. What's going on?"

"Not much. I haven't seen you in a while," he said.

"Yeah, I know. Everything all right?"

"Terrific."

There was a slight pause as she heard him rustle papers and then he continued, his voice lowered: "That psychiatrist Dr. Lambdin sent Talia to is a weird S.O.B."

"You think everyone is weird. What's his name?"

"Panighetti. You know him?"

"I know of him. He has a good reputation; well respected."

"He better be. He wants to see her twice a week at seventy dollars a shot."

"What are you bellyaching about? You have insurance."

"Well, I'm not exactly sure I can use it for this." His voice changed again, becoming more guarded.

"Oh, I see." Carolyn laughed softly into the phone. "Don't want people at the office to know your wife is seeing a shrink; right?"

"Don't start analyzing. I'm just not sure I can use the insurance for this."

"Oh, no, of course not."

"His office is down on Peachtree, not far from yours. A little hole of a place; looks like he's been there fifty years. And he looks like he sleeps in his suit. I tell you, Carolyn, this guy is strange."

"Has he diagnosed the problem yet?"

"He said she was suffering from severe superego and something about possible schizophrenia."

"Anything else?"

"That's all he said. I'm supposed to meet with him after one of her sessions next week."

"How is Talia reacting?"

"I don't know." He sounded tired. "Angry, I guess. Maybe more withdrawn."

"What about the eating?"

"Same. Panighetti says we should let her go on as she's been. I don't think she's eaten anything in the last two days. Do you think that's good?"

"I'm sure he's going about this in the way he thinks

best." When her voice sounded unconvincing, even to herself, Carolyn added: "Mike, don't worry. I'm sure he knows what he's doing."

After hanging up the phone Carolyn pressed the buzzer on her desk, a signal for her secretary.

"Did you want me, Dr. Stepler?" A pleasant, curly-headed, dark-skinned girl smiled as she opened the door to Carolyn's inner office. Freddie, short for Frederika, had been with Carolyn since she opened her practice.

"Freddie, I need you to do some legwork for me."

"Sure."

"First of all I want you to order these books." Carolyn handed the young woman a slip of paper torn from a memo pad; two titles were scrawled across the sheet. "I don't know the names of the publishing companies, but both books are written by Dr. Hilde Bruch, a professor of psychiatry at Baylor. Call Houston if need be to find them, but I want those books, the sooner the better. Next," Carolyn said, tearing another page from the pad, "I want you to go to the med-school library at Emory. Find me every piece of information you can on this subject. Look in all the most recent psychiatric journals; don't bother going back any further than the last five years. Make copies of everything and bring it all back here."

"All right," Freddie said, making notes.

"Then," said Carolyn, "call the psychiatric division over at Emory and ask if they've had any recent cases of anorexia. If not, try Piedmont, Grady, West Paces Ferry, or any of the other hospitals in town. I want to talk with anyone who's handled or been associated with a patient who has this disorder."

"Is this the one where they starve themselves?"

"Exactly." She smiled at Freddie and gave her a twenty-dollar bill to cover the cost of photocopies at the library. "Start giving me any information as soon as you get it."

"Right."

Freddie took the bill and placed it in her pocket.

"Dr. Stepler, we don't have a patient with this problem, do we?"

"No, Fred. Just a friend."

=== 12 ===

Why were we not informed?" Mother demanded.

"Joan, I was going to phone you in a few days." It was Michael who spoke now. "When I knew a little more. I didn't want you to worry is all."

Talia watched Michael carefully from her corner near the fireplace without fire. He still stood at the door, hands stuffed in his pockets, foraging, she knew, for confidence but only finding coins. He appeared suddenly awkward; a lone pawn preciously positioned on an undefended square.

Father slowly advanced, masterfully preparing to decimate the opposing force.

Mother moved not to Michael, but to Talia, placing a sovereign hand on Talia's arm; the calculating power knowing which pawn can be safely captured and which, for now, should be left alone.

"How do you feel, Talia?" Mother said, tightening her hold. Talia pulled loose, retreating further into her corner, and followed, only visually, the choreography of dust particles darting freely to the window from a patch of sunlight on the floor. She tried desperately to find an answer to Mother's question. There was none. Mother would have done as well to ask it of the ascending composition of atmosphere within that descending column of light.

"Your appearance is awful. Look at her, Louis."

"I see her," said Father, glaring at Michael. "Your fly is down, young man," he added and portentously turned around.

Talia had known they would come; known it more

assuredly than any other thought which had ever registered in her mind. She had known it last night; Mother had called promptly at eight, her usual Saturday night investigation: "I'm not disturbing you?" Mother had started out.

"No, Mother."

"You haven't plans for the evening?"

"No."

"I would have phoned later then, when the rates are lower, had I known."

The questioning would continue until it debarked, as it always did, on the matter of Talia's future. Only last night Talia could endure the subject no longer and said:

"I don't want to discuss it, Mother."

"You've given no thought to a career?"

"No," Talia had said.

"And you're not planning to return to school?"

"I don't *know*, Mother."

"Well, what *are* you doing, child?"

"Seeing a psychiatrist," and Talia quietly replaced the receiver on the phone.

They had arrived this morning before nine. She was preparing batter for Michael's waffles, had just folded in pecans, when she heard the car in the drive. Michael had put down the Sunday paper and walked to the kitchen window, letting up the shade.

"Ah, shit!" he had said. "It's them."

"Who?" said Talia, knowing.

"Your goddamned parents," and he had run upstairs to dress.

Father and Mother were standing opposite one another now as Mother ran a hand through Talia's hair. The muscles in Talia's stomach were contracting; a serpentine bed of knots.

"She is ill," Michael was saying in a whisper.

"I have eyes." Father moved closer to the opposition. "I realize there is a problem. But there is nothing wrong with my daughter's mind."

"When has she last eaten?" Mother said, studying a strand of Talia's hair.

Michael ignored the question and addressed Father: "The physician said her condition is psychological. There is nothing physically wrong."

"Who? Who did you take her to that would tell you such a thing?" Mother interrogated, letting the strand fall, jerking her hand to her side.

"A Dr. Lambdin. He was recommended by a friend."

"Which in itself tells us reams." Father walked to the sofa, picked up a cushion and examined the chintz. "The friend of one mirrors the other."

It was Mother's move: "I asked you to send her to Dr. Abelard."

Michael countered: "She no longer lives in Athens, Joan. She is my wife now, and I did what I thought best."

"He would have put her on an accelerated diet, maybe, or medication," said Mother. "But Dr. Abelard would not have sent a Sinclaire to a psychiatrist. Absolutely not."

"Dr. Lambdin felt psychiatry was the only route," said Michael.

"Glandular. It has to be glandular."

"I told you, Joan, Talia underwent a complete physical. Lambdin found nothing organically wrong."

"What about the low blood pressure? And what else was it? Something about metabolism?"

"Low basal metabolic rate." Talia enunciated carefully. The others turned to her and stared.

"Whatever that means." Mother turned to Michael, dismissing the remark. "What's he doing about it?"

"He feels those things are a result of the weight loss, not the cause. And he believes they will correct themselves eventually."

"Glandular," Mother stated, returning to Talia's hair. She repeated the word several times to herself.

"Exactly what *is* it this quack is doing for her?" Father said. "She looks worse than ever."

"His name is Dr. Panighetti. And we're going to have to be patient. This kind of thing obviously takes time."

"A Sinclaire has never stepped inside a psychiatrist's office until now, Michael. *Never.* Our minds are as sound as . . ." Father looked about the room as if searching for some tangible parallel. " *'Orandum est ut sit mens sana in corpore sano,'* " he said at last and began loading his pipe. Talia translated silently; Father must be out of parallels, she decided.

Mother moved closer now, invading, taking Talia's hand. "A psychiatrist, indeed! The whole thing is beyond the absurd. I think we should take her home."

"This is home, goddamn it," Michael said, his face tight, the color and texture of a wild plum. "If you would both think of Talia for two seconds instead of yourselves—"

"Young man, I'll have you know—"

This time Father was interrupted by Mother. "She is *all* we think about. How dare you criticize us?"

"The irony of parenting, my dear," Father said placidly to Mother. Then to Talia: "What do *you* think of what your Michael is doing, Talia Victoria?"

Talia looked at Father squarely. " 'Minds are in a state of slavery,' " she said, mounting the static cycle and beginning to pedal. " 'Rebel, think of yourself, let others grumble. Dare to be singular—let others sleep.' "

They all stared.

"Well, what the hell is that supposed to mean?" said Father softly, shifting his head back and forth from Mother to Michael.

"Alcott," Talia intoned as she pedaled. "Simply Bronson Alcott, Father."

She turned to Michael. He was still watching her, eyes gentle, and for a moment, she thought he was going to smile.

●　　●　　●

Carolyn sipped hot tea brought in a thermos from home. She had been at the office since seven. She often did this, driving into town on Sunday mornings long before the rest of the planet was stirred back to life. It seemed to give her a jump on humanity; it separated and set her above the rest.

She walked to the window and drew up the blinds. There was still little movement down below. Peachtree and Spring streets were empty except for an occasional derelict left over from Saturday night. From her seventh-story window she looked down on the still-sleeping Atlanta and was alone.

It had taken time and a not inconsiderable amount of pain to realize it, but it was wise to be alone. She had been raised by parents whom she had been taught to call Maria and Dan since the age of two. They were born first cousins in a large family of medical men. Maria was first rebuked by the clan when she wanted to join the ranks of the opposite gender and was totally disowned when she married Dan. "We liked each other more than anyone else we knew," Carolyn's mother was proud of telling. "It seemed appropriate that we should marry." The ceremony had taken place in their last year at the University of Pennsylvania Medical School with only their friends in attendance. But the repudiation of their family seemed to disunite the two rather than draw them closer together. They separated when Carolyn was three, both denying their lack of divorce had anything to do with the family being Catholic, and had remained so over the past thirty years. Their shared interests seemed to be the love of their profession and the fact that they had produced a biological perfection in Carolyn. She had often wondered, now that she was older, if her birth had been merely a study in homozygous genetics. At any rate, whatever their reasoning, Carolyn had remained an only child.

She had lived with her mother in New Jersey during the winters and, when she reached high school, stayed with her father during the summers in his apartment in

New York. Occasionally the family was together on weekends; at least Dan brought his shaving gear home. But each member, all participants in the post-Freudian generation, went his own way. It was one of Carolyn's first lessons in independence.

The second came while she was in college. On holidays her parents started traveling. The first Christmas they went to Bermuda. The second year they flew to France. "This way," Maria had explained, "you're not tethered by any kind of filial guilt. You're free to go and do as you please." So while her parents sojourned about the globe, permitting her "freedom," she sat in Poughkeepsie, the envy of her family-harnessed roommates, and cried.

Carolyn let the blinds back down and returned to her desk. It was a clutter of photocopies Freddie had made; reports from the *American Journal of Psychiatry, Psychoneuroendocrinology,* and the *Journal of Psychosomatic Research*. She took another swallow of tea and returned to the material. The first of the books Freddie ordered had arrived Friday and Carolyn had finally begun reading it this morning. She was now a third of the way through the small, clearly written text.

She was intrigued by what she read. Anorexia nervosa was a debilitating dysfunction which rarely affected men. Its victims were nearly always girls, or young women, from upper middle class, highly educated families. She began making a list of symptoms as she read and then making a note to the side if it was one she knew Talia had. The others, the ones she was not positive of, she would ask Mike about.

Mike. She laid the book aside and considered him a moment. The last few weeks she had thought of him often; too much. When she was with him, she dreaded the time when he would leave. When she was alone, she was continually tempted to pick up the phone. She had never felt this way about a man, had never allowed herself to feel this way. It wasn't love; she was fairly certain there wasn't such a thing. Possibly Mike was a physical distraction. She had learned that psychiatry demanded escape; to forget what transpired during the hours at the office, to dislodge the horrors that filtered into her brain from other troubled minds, she had to concentrate fully on what she did at any given moment. When she bathed, she thought of nothing else. She became aware of only the water, the soap, and her body. Her mother, a psychiatrist also, had taken it a step further. No matter what the New Jersey weather, Maria worked several hours each evening with her bromeliads and begonias in a small greenhouse she had built onto the garage. "I would drown in a sea of insanity without this," Maria used to say, her hands in soiled cotton gloves, working with a mud-covered spade. She had won first prize for her *Begonia rex*, "*Vesuvias*," two years in a row, and prided herself on having the finest *Aechmea fasciatas* in the state. Maria's escape was horticulture. Carolyn's, apparently, was Mike.

On their second date, which ended at her apartment, she had told him she never became serious about anyone. "Good," he had said, grinning as he played with his wedding band. "Neither do I." She had liked that; liked his liking that their arrangement did not include attachment. Other men wanted her to live with them or, worse, marry. The ones who did not were frightened by her independence, her profession, and her income which usually surpassed their own. Mike, on the other hand, reveled in her female emancipation, her aggression, and, mostly, her money.

When it began eight months ago, their affair had been casual, fun. But since their trip to Miami the relationship had changed. The problem with Talia was wearing on him and he was continually tired and worried. The thing that bothered Carolyn was that Mike was troubled and she honestly cared.

She tried not to think about it now. Concentrate! she told herself. She read through the next several pages of her book. The anorexic patient begins to starve herself, Carolyn learned, apparently as a desperate search for autonomy. The patient acts to control her body when she feels she controls nothing else.

Carolyn had first heard of anorexia when she was in college. Her mother had worked with a patient then, for four or five months, who had the disorder. Maria had felt they were progressing when the parents of the girl withdrew her from therapy. Carolyn considered phoning Maria; she would want to know details: patient's weight, background, duration of amenorrhea, proposed method of treatment. Carolyn debated momentarily, then decided, emphatically, she should not call. She had been taught to be independent; no point in falling parasitic to her mother's experience now.

She had returned to the book when she heard a drawer being opened and closed in the outer office. She looked at her watch; it would be Freddie. Carolyn had sent her to the Georgia State Mental Institution in Milledgeville on Saturday. Freddie was to see if she could obtain any information on an anorexic patient that had been treated there. She and Carolyn were then to meet here this morning at ten.

"Hi," Freddie called, sticking her head around the door. She was dressed in jeans, her hair pinned at the crown and falling in tendrils around her face and neck.

"You're early," Carolyn said.

"I knew you'd already be here. I couldn't wait to give you all this stuff."

"You found something?"

"*Beaucoup!* They've had several cases of this thing in the past few years. I talked to one doctor who believes it's on the increase. Almost epidemic among a certain class of people."

"That's what I've been reading. What else did you find?"

"I talked with a nurse who worked with two cases. They were female and both patients had drastic weight loss before being hospitalized. An average of . . ." she fumbled through her notes, "an average of forty-two pounds. The head nurse let me see the case histories after I gave her your letter. I wrote down weight gain, weight loss, mental attitude, body temperature, everything." She handed a spiral notebook to Carolyn.

"Thanks, Freddie. You did a good job," Carolyn said.

"Thanks." She picked up her jacket, then turned at the door. "Dr. Stepler?"

"Yes, Freddie."

"I saw a photograph of one of those girls. She weighed fifty-nine pounds. It was terrible. Dr. Stepler, she died."

=== 13 ===

"Well, find out or we're in trouble!" Mike's voice could be heard in the hall.

Carolyn pushed open the door to his office, which was already ajar. He stood in front of his desk, his back to her, a telephone receiver clamped between shoulder and ear. Speaking in sharp, staccato replies, he probed through the folders and stacks of paper spread across his desk. There was a slight stain running vertically down the back of his shirt, and his hair was uncharacteristically out of place. Carolyn made two swift raps against the door and edged her way inside the vortex of paper, people, and coalescing voices.

A slight woman, overpowered by a bright canopy of red hair, looked up from the desk when Carolyn knocked. She whispered something to Mike, then continued helping him sort through the clutter. Mike waved one of his assistants out of the only chair in the room, and motioned for Carolyn to sit.

"All right," he said. "Call me back." He glanced at Carolyn briefly while holding up a hand as if to keep her silent. He addressed his secretary: "Get me those reports, Sue," and then, as if on a second thought: "and check the teletype again."

"What's the excitement?" Carolyn said.

"The stock—" he halted, interrupted by the ringing of another phone. "Freeman," he snapped. "When? How much?" As he listened he wrapped the coiling wire from the receiver around his fingers. His mouth was tight and he stared ahead as if furious at the opposite wall. "I know that," he said sharply. "Well, I'm trying, damn it, I'm trying!" He slammed down the phone.

"Heard a stock report lately?" He removed his coat from the back of Carolyn's chair. His shirt sleeves were rolled but his tie was still fastidiously in place. "The whole damn bottom is falling out."

The secretary returned, a stack of computerized printouts in hand.

"Anything?" said Mike.

"No, sir."

"Did you try his house again?"

"No one there."

"All right, check all outgoing flights since yesterday afternoon. If he left town, I want to know where he is." He turned to Carolyn as the girl walked out. "Stoner," he said, as if to explain.

"How did Talia's session go yesterday?" Carolyn crossed her legs.

"What?"

"Your wife. Did you take her to Panighetti?"

"Oh, yeah. Yeah." He was thumbing through papers again. "The son-of-a-bitch has left town."

"Panighetti?"

"Hell, no. Stoner. Frank Stoner. He announced a possible merger with Intercon yesterday at the board meeting. Our stock's dropped fifteen points since the exchange opened this morning and now the bastard's nowhere to be found."

"Has Panighetti diagnosed her problem yet, Mike?" The phone rang again.

"Hello!" he answered quickly. "Right. Right! I don't know; I don't think so. Not yet." The secretary came in, waving to gain his attention, and then mouthed a message to Mike. "Tell him *no way*," he mouthed back. She ran from the room like a messenger ant darting in and out of a hole.

"Have you talked to Rhoades?" Mike asked of the phone. "Yeah, they're all hot down here too. All right, get back to me." He put a finger on the button, then removed it to punch out a seven-digit number on the panel.

"How *is* Talia, Mike?"

"A second," he said, pointing a finger. "Eliot, what's happening?" He ran a hand through his hair. "I know exactly what it means. Well, keep trying."

He hung up, exhaled loudly, expanding his cheeks, and then looked at Carolyn. "You want some coffee or something?" he said and walked to the door. "Sue!"

"No, none for me, thanks," Carolyn said. "I was asking how Talia is doing."

"Talia? Yeah, she's fine, I guess. Fine."

"Has Dr. Panighetti diagnosed her problem yet?"

"Sue, get Dr. Stepler here some coffee, will you?" he said when the secretary returned.

"Yes, sir." The redhead stared at Carolyn, obviously annoyed.

A man, the one whose seat Carolyn had usurped, appeared at the door just as the secretary was leaving.

"Was Stoner on any of the flights?" Mike asked him. "Have you found out anything?"

"I'm trying," he said and exited.

"Mike, I want to talk to you about Talia."

"Not now, Carolyn." He turned his back to her, picked up a file, then turned back around. "What are you doing here, anyway? Don't you have patients?"

"I brought in a report I've been doing for personnel. I decided to stop in."

"Can we meet later? Your place? I'll—"

"Well, we've located him!" A very junior attorney Carolyn had met at a party last fall barged through the door. "Stoner caught a flight to New York City last night."

"And he didn't say where he was going?"

"Not that we know. What do you make of it?"

Michael dug into his pockets. "I don't know. But something's going on."

"Should we try to find out where he's staying?"

"No. Stoner built this fire. Maybe this time we'll get to watch him fry."

"You think he'll pull off the merger?"

"If he stands to benefit from it, you can bet he'll try. Call the board members and set up a meeting for this afternoon around four."

"You can't, Mr. Freeman," Mike's secretary said. "You have a meeting scheduled with attorneys representing the victims of that crash in South Carolina last year. They'll be here at four."

"Get Bruce to handle that."

"Mike, that meeting is crucial," the fellow lawyer said.

"Bruce can handle it. Tell them I'm sick. Tell them I died."

With the others out of the room now, Mike again reached for the phone, then halted. "Why did you say you were here?"

"A personality profile I developed for personnel."

"Oh, yeah. Listen, I'm pretty busy right now," he said.

"Mike, is Talia's attitude better?"

"I think so; more or less. Why the interest?"

"Curiosity. I wondered how things were going."

"How about letting me call you tonight? We'll go to dinner or—ah, damn!" He reached for the phone. "Are you kidding?" he said. "*Here?* Ah, damn! No, send them in." He cradled the receiver. "Shit."

"What is it?" Carolyn said.

"Just sit there, don't say a thing." He stood and pulled on his coat, shirt sleeves still rolled. He cleared his throat and straightened an already plumb tie.

The door to Mike's office was thrown open as a tall, slender woman in her early fifties entered. She was followed by a man who appeared fifteen years older and who, although actually taller, seemed shorter because of his broad neck and shoulders.

"Hello, Joan." Mike bent, kissing the cheek she proffered. And then: "Dr. Sinclaire," he said, shaking the man's hand. "This is a surprise."

"We have been with Talia," the woman didn't hesitate. "Michael, I want to take her home."

"Joan, we discussed this last week." Mike eased back against a filing cabinet. He, too, seemed shortened by the erectness of the woman.

"She is worse. Can you not see that?"

"A man sees what he wants to see," the elder man said. "I thought you had learned that of Michael by now." He withdrew a parcel of tobacco from a coat pocket.

"I have been *told*," Mike said, not looking at Carolyn, "that it is normal for a disturbed patient to get worse before getting better."

"It is that very attitude that I admonish," said the woman. "Our daughter is not disturbed. I refuse to recognize the word."

"Joan, all I meant was that we mustn't be impatient."

"You said that last week."

" 'The man who never alters his opinion is like standing water, and breeds serpents of the mind.' " Dr. Sinclaire turned pompously, his little arms in the air, reminding Carolyn of a great auk who thinks he has performed well and seeks the commendation of others.

"Michael, I'm sure you have meant well. I am even willing to forget what has transpired," said Talia's mother.

"He means to seek power, my dear. Tyrant of the children."

Mike said: "When are you going to get it through your head that Talia is no longer a child?"

"Actually, she is," said the mother. "Talia has remained immature."

The phone rang again, and Mike went to the desk. "Yes?" he answered. "No, let me call you back."

As he spoke, Mrs. Sinclaire turned to Carolyn and scrutinized. Carolyn turned the pages of a notebook and pretended to read.

"I apologize for the interruption," Mike said. "Things are hectic today. Perhaps you could drive back to the house and as soon as I finish here, we'll all go for dinner and discuss this."

"As far as I'm concerned, it's settled," said Mrs. Sinclaire. "I want to take her home. Three weeks in Athens and she'll be fine again."

"Did Talia say she wanted to go?"

"Talia cannot know what is best for her right now. This is a decision a mother must make."

"Joan, we have to give this a chance. A little more time in therapy and she'll—"

"That's what's wrong with her now. That psychiatrist has her so confused she doesn't know what is happening. She doesn't know what she's saying."

"Joan, let me set up an appointment with Dr. Panighetti so he can explain his procedures to you."

"Forget that, young man." It was the father. "My wife and I will not endorse this nonsense."

"Dr. Sinclaire, *sir*," the tone was biting. "I suggest it so you both might have a better understanding of Talia's problem and what Dr. Panighetti is struggling to accomplish."

The telephone interrupted him once more.

"Ah, damn. Sue! Get that," Mike said and ignored the phone.

"I understand that Talia is starving," the mother's voice rose. "She is losing weight. Losing instead of gaining. She looks horrible; it's an embarrassment. That doctor has done *nothing* to get her to eat."

"I know that, Joan."

"Then why do you keep sending her to this man?"

"Because I have to assume he knows more about this than I do. And Panighetti says weight gain will occur when he's uncovered her psychological problems."

"She has no psychological problems except ones he's putting in her head! He's made her believe she wants to have her father's child! It's *obscene*."

"He hasn't said that," Mike said.

"That is exactly what Talia told me this morning. I want to take her home. Let Dr. Abelard tell me what is wrong."

"Joan, you know she's been to a physician."

"I want to take her home."

Mike's secretary entered, an excited expression on her birdlike face.

"What is it, Sue?"

"It's about Frank Stoner, Mr. Freeman." Mike nodded for her to go ahead. "He's been named chief legal advisor at Intercontinental. They just announced it in New York."

Mike massaged his eyes. "Okay, Sue."

"I don't recall that we were through, Michael."

"I'm taking her home." The mother's expression was set.

"No, Joan, you are not." Carolyn thought Mike's hands trembled; his words were even. "She is staying where she is. And I'm going to do what I think best."

"That's the way you choose to play this game?" said Talia's father.

"This is not a goddamned game!"

"He wants to be in control here, Joan. Let's go."

"No! Not until I know what's going to be done."

"Yes, you will go home, Joan," said Mike. "And from now on whatever happens is my responsibility. I am Talia's husband, damn you. She is not a *child*. She's my wife, got that? My legally wedded adult wife."

A tense, painful silence followed the Sinclaires' departure. Carolyn spoke first:

"It's not going to work, you know."

"What won't work?" Mike snapped.

"Talia's therapy with Panighetti. It isn't working."

"Well, great. That's fantastic. You're the one who told me to take her to a damn psychiatrist in the first place!"

"And you should. But apparently not Panighetti. He isn't using the right approach."

"Here I've been defending the man and he's wrong?"

"I've done some research on the subject. The therapy that fails is just what Panighetti seems to be doing."

Mike sighed. "Okay, so what do I do?"

"Take her to another psychiatrist. I'll recommend someone else to you."

"You heard her parents. They'll never go for another one."

"I thought you handled them pretty well."

He shrugged. "They'll be back."

"Mike, Talia is suffering from a severe eating disorder called anorexia nervosa. Her refusal to eat results from an extremely complex and deeply rooted psychological base. She needs help."

He sat on the edge of the desk, facing her, his shoulders bent. Finally: "Will you take her?"

"No."

"You know about this thing. This problem. You take her."

"No. That's not a good idea."

"But you understand what's wrong. You probably know more about her than another doctor could learn in weeks."

"I can't."

"Why not?"

"Well, for one thing, you and I."

"Carolyn, please. I need help. I don't know what else to do. She weighs less than seventy-five pounds. Joan's right, she *is* getting worse; she looks awful. I'm scared, Carolyn. *Really* scared. I need your help."

"If I do this—if I take Talia as a patient—you know what that does to us? You understand that; that our relationship would be over?"

She waited for his response, already knowing what it would be.

"Yes."

"And you want to do this, even though it means ending the things between you and me?"

"I want you to treat her."

Carolyn now sat behind Mike's desk and he sat in the lone, straight-backed chair against the wall of his office.

"We need to get a few things straight," she said, her

voice professional, direct. "Give me ten minutes without interruption and we can get this done."

He leaned forward and spoke into a speaker on his desk: "Hold all my calls for the next half hour. I want no interruptions. No," he said, soberly, "not even that."

Carolyn began, eyes on the paper in front of her, mind locking against distraction, discarding all fragments of the past. "Call Panighetti immediately," she said. "Tell him what you've decided. I'll phone him myself tomorrow and request Talia's file. I'll want to consult with the physician. Do you have his name?"

"Martin Lambdin," said Mike. "His office is in a medical building on Peachtree, next to Piedmont Hospital."

"A couple of things." She spoke quickly, tapping her pen against the desk. "First, you must be ready to accept the fact that this may take months, possibly years."

He nodded.

"After an initial consultation with you and her family, I may suggest there be no association with her parents for a while. From what I've seen today this may be difficult. It will be up to you to see that it is done.

"Next, I will want to see Talia two, maybe three times a week at the outset. My fees are comparable with other psychiatrists' in the area. You may discuss terms with my secretary if you like.

"I will more than likely prescribe a moderate diet, one suggested by Dr. Lambdin, that will not be too overwhelming to the patient. I will expect your full cooperation in helping Talia follow the program. Are there any questions?"

"Do you think you can help her?"

"I would not be doing this if I did not."

"Thank you," he said simply.

Carolyn moved to the door. "Have her in my office Thursday morning at nine."

=== 14 ===

"Thank you for seeing me, Dr. Lambdin," Carolyn said, seating herself at a small white table in the cafeteria of Piedmont Hospital.

The elderly, balding man smiled and transferred crackers and a bowl of soup to the table from tray. Liver spots dotted a slightly trembling hand.

"Sure you won't join me?" he said, pointing to the meal.

"No, thanks. This is fine." Carolyn sipped orange juice, then asked: "You only saw Mrs. Freeman the one time?"

"Never came back. Extremely hostile. The most anxious young woman I've seen in some time." He sucked a spoonful of soup, then muttered, "Ah, too hot!" while fanning his mouth. "When the patient came to me, and that has been six or seven weeks ago, she only weighed somthing like seventy-five, no . . ." he moved an arthritic finger down a page, ". . . no, seventy-six pounds. She was terribly evasive about previous weight, but according to her husband that represents a total loss of thirty-nine pounds over the last eleven months."

"Did you prescribe medication?"

" 'Provera,' to induce bleeding. It seems she's suffered amenorrhea almost since the time she began losing weight."

"Were there any other physical problems?"

"Not really. Sugar-tolerance curve was flat, and basal metabolic rate was low—a minus twenty-eight percent. Blood pressure was ninety-five over sixty, but

135

I feel those things will be improved as soon as her diet is corrected. They are by no means the cause of her weight loss. Cracker?" he offered.

She shook her head. "What about body temperature; was it low?"

"You've been doing your homework, doctor. Temperature was ninety-six degrees. You know . . ." he slurped the soup. "This is a very enigmatic case. One might think of Addison's disease because of the severe emaciation. But I had to discount it immediately because there was no pigmentation and certainly none of the characteristic weakness present. The contrary, in fact; she was extremely sharp and agile. Quite restless. I couldn't keep her still."

"You don't believe the illness is a result of an insufficiency of the anterior lobe of the pituitary gland?"

"No, I considered Simmonds' disease, but there was no tumor or trauma to the anterior lobe, and the patient has never given birth, which in that disease is generally the case. She looks much older than she should for her age, but there isn't nearly the marked appearance of senility you find in Simmonds'."

"And her secondary sexual characteristics?"

"All normal." He took several spoonfuls of soup, trickling it down his chin, and then a large, noisy swallow of milk. "No," he continued, "there was absolutely none of the atrophy you might expect of sexual organs. External genitalia was perfectly normal. Breasts normally developed and axillary and pubic hair abundant."

"Then you think the illness is an emotional one?"

"That's why I sent her over to Joe Panighetti. In my opinion it has to be psychological. For one thing, she refuses to admit she is ill. When I suggested the importance of eating, she balked. The only things she did complain of were dyspepsia and periodic pain in the epigastrium and lower abdomen." He drank the last of the soup and then stuffed cellophane packaging from the crackers into his empty bowl. "And she mentioned something about feeling 'full.' That was her reason for not eating, because of this continual, uncomfortable 'fullness.' "

"Again, I thank you," Carolyn said as they gathered used utensils from the table and returned them to the tray. "You've been a tremendous help to me, Dr. Lambdin."

"There's one thing I'd like to know," he said as they stood.

"Of course."

"Why is the patient's husband removing her from Joe's care?"

"Mr. Freeman believes a stalemate has been reached in his wife's therapy. Often, in a situation such as this, it's wise to have consultation with another psychiatrist or a change of therapist altogether."

"Joe believes this change is a grave error."

"Yes, sir, I know. I spoke with him yesterday."

"Is he wrong?"

"*I* think so. Mrs. Freeman, in my opinion, is suffering from an acute case of primary anorexia nervosa."

"I concur with that diagnosis," he said.

Carolyn smiled. "I hoped you would. You see, Dr. Panighetti feels Mrs. Freeman fears oral impregnation and is using amenorrhea as a psychological bastion against oedipal guilt. The anorexic patient has such complex and deep-seated psychological problems that I can understand why he was tempted to use the approach he did. But I also feel he was relying on concepts which are outmoded and which, in this case, could be fatal."

They walked outside, through the double doors of the cafeteria, toward the blue tile of the Sheffield Medical Building.

"Dr. Stepler," he stopped, and in the sunlight sad yellow patches of chloasma were revealed on his face and head. "Have you seen Mrs. Freeman yet?"

"No, sir, I haven't."

"I spent four months on the U.S.S. *Hope* back in 1965. I had expected, and was therefore able to cope with, human suffering and physical devastation of impoverished peoples. I was ready to accept the malnutrition and the slow, painful deaths caused by starvation that I saw. But, doctor, I was not ready to see, in Atlanta, Georgia, among wealth and prosperity, what I saw when that young woman walked through my office door. I hope you are prepared."

She was not.

Carolyn had arrived at her office Thursday morning before six. Unable to sleep Wednesday night, she had taken hot baths; imbibed warm milk; extinguished lights and listened to Brahms. Nothing had helped. She had tried to read, only to find herself distracted and suddenly realizing she knew not at all what she had read for scores of pages.

At last, unable to tolerate her wrestle with consciousness and her campaign for sleep any longer, she had risen from bed, showered, prepared a light breakfast, and started into town by twenty after five.

For the next several hours she studied all the notes about Talia she had made over the last few weeks. The bits and pieces of information Mike had given her concerning eating habits, rituals, family background, scraps of dialogue. She went diligently through data given her by Dr. Lambdin; scrutinized every morsel she had obtained from Panighetti: Talia's response to Rorschach testing, his interpretations of Talia's fantasies and dreams, his claims that she had a "negativistic attitude" and that she defied "any kind of perception or understanding."

She probed through psychological journals; analyzed the case histories Freddie had retrieved from Milledgeville; and examined again what had become her Bible, the book on eating disorders written by the world's foremost authority on anorexia, Dr. Hilde Bruch.

She assured herself she could handle this case; that she would not make the mistakes many therapists, including her mother, had made in treating this illness.

And she tried to forearm herself for the worst, to prepare for the sight of Talia Freeman.

Despite herself, she was shocked.

The figure which stood inside the closed door of Carolyn's office possessed the body of a child, the face of a much older woman. The facial skin was dry and flaccid, sunken and accentuated by drastically edged cheekbones; her thin, shriveled lips were overpowered by a fiercely honed nose; dark, retreating eyes were chased by thick ebony brows. Angular shoulders and elbows jutted through the folds of her blouse, and pitifully thin legs were exposed beneath the hem of her skirt. The outfit was drawn tight at the waist by an oversized belt. The physical appearance of this woman—her dull, ocherous skin and withered hair; her emaciated legs, dramatized by the protruding caps of her knees—seemed to warrant the aid of a wheelchair or the need to be carried, the fragile body laid gently in bed. But instead the figure stood emphatically erect, eyes darting wildly about the room.

Carolyn walked from behind her desk.

"I'm Dr. Stepler," she said. As she extended a hand, Talia shrank, her eyes alert and focused on Carolyn. "You may sit if you wish," Carolyn offered as she herself took a seat in a grouping of four comfortably upholstered chairs.

"I stand." The voice was strong, lucid; nothing Carolyn had imagined could come from someone so frail.

"Talia? May I call you Talia or do you prefer Mrs. Freeman?"

"It's your office."

"All right. I shall call you Talia. Why do you think you're here, Talia?"

"To waste a great deal of money and time on idiotic chatter."

"Is that the way you felt about your sessions with Dr. Panighetti?"

Silence. Talia paced up and down the room, long strides athletically stretching across the floor. Her look was defiant as she glared at Carolyn.

"Talia, you and I can work together. But our first task is to help you regain some of your weight."

"I am *sick*, sick of everyone telling me to eat!" Talia's hands were tight in front of her as she marched nearer. "It is not going to make it all better—just because I eat."

"I agree."

"It's my body."

"Indeed it is. It is also your mind and we must coordinate treatment of both."

Talia returned to her pacing: quick, regimented steps.

"Talia, do you know what anorexia nervosa is?" Carolyn followed the stalking movements of her patient, a stick marionette. "It's an illness, Talia."

Talia continued across the room, her steps those of a demanding soldier.

"I don't know your thoughts, Talia, but I know patients with your condition use dieting as a form of self-control. They do it because they think they are weak, or inferior, or because they fear they may not reach the expectations of their parents, or husbands, or friends. They do it because they're afraid of failing. They do it as a check on their lives; to prove they are strong. Starvation raises them above the less articulate masses and makes them special. It is not really being thin that's so important, but the control over their bodies that results in being thin."

Talia was standing still now, listening.

"The unhappy part is that anorexic patients want to be healthy and strong while proving they are in control. Then their strength begins to fade. They are no longer healthy. But, you see, they like this because they keep fighting; they are still in control. And the resulting illness gains attention."

"That's not true! I wouldn't do that! I've always been a perfect child. Ask my mother—she'll tell you I had a perfect childhood."

"Were you happy as a child?"

Talia began her march anew.

"What about school, Talia? Did you enjoy school?"

The defiance returned; Talia looked straight ahead as she sliced through the room.

"Some patients, even though they do well in school, feel badly for not having done better. They feel guilty for not having been absolutely the best or because they wished to do other things with their lives than what they thought was expected of them; what their parents wanted. The suffering which comes from not eating is a punishment of themselves. They put a prohibition on pleasure because of guilt.

"But they also experience anger for having to push themselves, for always having to study, to do the right things. And denying themselves what *they* want. Then they end up in this terrible struggle, this—"

"Dichotomy," said, Talia, halting.

"Yes. And then they begin to feel that they don't know what it is they want. They're confused, and soon food is the only thing they think about. Other people who have had this illness, Talia, they felt that maybe they did not have a mind of their own. They complied with all their parents' wishes, did everything expected of them."

"I did exactly what they wanted. Always."

"Sometimes parents of these other girls made them feel guilty because they gave them so much; gave things the girls didn't really want. But they didn't want to disappoint their parents by telling them this. Have you ever felt that way, Talia?"

Rather than answering Talia sat, leaving an empty chair between herself and Carolyn.

"You see, Talia, these other anorexic girls didn't know what it would take to make them happy. So they kept on dieting. It became the most important thing in their lives, because it made them feel they had obtained complete control; it made them feel they had obtained something special."

"It *is* special."

"Is that the way you feel? That it makes you special?"

"You tell me. You're the one who is supposed to know."

"I don't know, Talia. Your mind is your own, very singular and rare."

Talia said, almost in a whisper, "My mother knows what I think. And sometimes Michael."

"Or do you think maybe it seems that way?"

"She does. Mother knows."

"Talia, many of the girls first said they liked being thin. But later, they said they hated it. It was terrible. Cold and painful. More than anything else they wanted food and wanted to be comfortable and warm again. These other girls—they're well now—they learned that pain is not an answer to their problems. They realized starving is not a solution."

Talia crossed her arms over her chest, her long, bony hands grasping gossamer sleeves.

"We deserve more than punishment and guilt out of life, Talia."

"I don't."

"Why do you say that?"

"I quit school."

"Maybe you need time to decide if you want to continue your studies. There's nothing wrong with taking a respite."

"Time is not to waste."

"If it helps you reach a mature decision, then it isn't a waste, is it?"

"I cannot waste—I cannot have failure."

"Many of those others I was talking about, they felt the same way. They had to be better than all the others. But they also said it was very lonely at the top. Isolated; all by themselves."

"Yes."

"Is that the way you feel?"

"It's a price one must pay."

"Perhaps you don't have to pay any price at all."

"Nothing is free."

"Talia, none of us should have to suffer to be happy." Carolyn leaned toward Talia, smiling. "You're a wonderful individual, Talia, without the starving. And when you realize that, you're going to get well."

═══ 15 ═══

Carolyn held a photograph in each hand. One, curled at the edges, with aged tape marking one side, was completely torn in half; the other, newer and cleaner, had corners crisp and flat. One was in color, the other black and white.

The former, a snapshot of a young woman in her early twenties, was taken at close range. The composition was unfortunate, the photographer too close to subject, the woman appearing too large for the frame. She held two objects; a small bouquet of crimson flowers and the hand of a person lost to the other half. The dress, off the shoulders, revealed the body of a well-developed, athletic female. Her hair was neatly combed and rounded about the face, catching hints of outdoor light in the gentle curving strands. The face was delicate and shy, the sun promising to burn the white skin, and a smile caused pleasant creases at the eyes and mouth.

The black and white exposure, shot from a distance, showed a tall, lank woman caught in movement, photographed unaware. Hands were pugilistic; tight balls of fists held next to a flat, prepubertal-looking breast. Legs were widely extended, the left stretched far beyond the right, and through layers of dark clothing protruded the caps of her knees. Hair was unctuous and separated; pressed slick and damp against the brow. Facial expression was tense, the mouth drawn straight and tight; eyes ebon and severe. Skin was dry and pallid; cheeks deeply recessed.

At their last session together, Talia had opened an

envelope and placed the photographs in Carolyn's hand:

"I brought these because I thought, possibly, you might be able to tell," Talia had said in the slow, soft whisper which over the last ten weeks had become her mien.

"Tell what, Talia?"

"A difference," she had said, staring at the snapshots. "I've been told my appearance has changed. But when I look at these, I'm unable to tell."

Carolyn held them out now, in front of her, as if to balance the two, these objects used to mirror but taken of a person who could no longer reflect.

She placed the old photograph on top of the new, slid them into the creased and faded envelope Talia had brought, and then tucked the envelope inside the large, bulging folder which had grown into Talia's file.

"I'm ready," Carolyn said into the phone. "You may send them in." She then stood, bracing herself against the firm support of her desk.

Talia's mother sat straight and tall, armed with a stoic demeanor; a fine white face and sharp, proud features were held elegantly erect.

The father, seated next to his wife, sank into his chair, his face settling down on the thick, broad neck.

"I don't mind telling you, Doctor, we do not like the idea of being here," Joan Sinclaire said, crossing one long, lean leg in front of the other.

"We'll make it as painless as possible," said Carolyn, looking ahead at the textbook example of American upper-middle-class, college-educated mother. "The main reason for you being here is to help Talia. With your assistance, we can obtain a clear picture of Talia's place within the family structure, and gain some insight of her life as a child."

"There's certainly no mystery there." Mrs. Sinclaire flicked a small piece of lint from her dress, then stood and brushed the seat of her chair. "Anyone in Athens could easily synopsize that."

"Please, tell me yourself," said Carolyn.

"The Sinclaires are regarded as a closely knit, extremely amicable family Totally *en rapport.* Do I know you from somewhere, Doctor?" The woman made a quick survey of Carolyn's dress.

"No, not likely." Carolyn studied her notes, then turned to the father. "Is that also the way you would describe your family? Amicable. Close. Harmonious?"

The man drew himself up, took a pipe from the pocket of his coat and started to reply.

"Of course it's the way he would describe the Sinclaires," Mrs. Sinclaire said. "Everyone does. Did you study at our university, perhaps?"

"I graduated from Vassar, Mrs. Sinclaire."

"Luckily, our children were educated in the South. They, of course, could have gone North if they had wanted. Harvard literally *begged* James to come to Boston."

"Because I went there." Louis Sinclaire sat taller in his seat, mouthing his pipe. " 'A human being is not, in any proper sense, a human being till he is educated.' Horace Mann."

"Not merely because you went to Harvard, Louis. James was a brilliant child."

"Describe Talia for me; her qualities." Carolyn took a chair opposite the Sinclaires.

"Our youngest daughter. She has given us nothing but pleasure, at least until now. You can, of course, understand our distress at this horrendous change."

"How would you describe Talia's childhood, Mrs. Sinclaire?"

"Happy and serene. A delightful child."

"Never any problems?"

"Always serene. I've saved letters from her teachers since kindergarten; they fairly worshipped her, Louis, wouldn't you say?"

"Yes; very good child."

"She never gave you any trouble? Never mischievous; never did anything wrong?"

"A perfect child until this 'illness' came."

"Don't you think that unusual, Mrs. Sinclaire? For a growing child never once to be out of line?"

"We were the envy of our friends."

"You said your family is close?"

The mother nodded.

"Would you say too close, perhaps?"

"What am I to take that to mean?"

"Most patients with anorexia come from families which are *intensely* close. This in itself can be the root of the problem. A child protected by a solicitous family is often unable to reach a normal state of independence."

Mrs. Sinclaire shifted. "You make it sound as if it were wrong to have created a warm, loving home for our children."

"I don't mean to imply that at all."

"The implication was certainly there." She turned from Carolyn and straightened the hem of her dress. "You might be interested to know, Doctor, that Louis and I are regarded by our friends as devoted parents. I was once selected by the Athens PTA as Mother of the Year."

"Tell me, did Talia have many friends as a child?"

"All our children were quite popular."

"Did she have many friends?"

"She might not have socialized as often as, say, some of the more—fatuous girls. Talia enjoyed her home."

"Did you select Talia's friends?"

"Indeed not." She reshifted. "Is this an investigation?"

"Talia mentioned that you disapproved of her one close friend."

"It is the function of a parent to guide." Louis Sinclaire stood and walked to the bookcase. "I, as a father, have had to take it upon myself to steer our children in the proper direction. It is not so much a matter of disapproving."

"Besides," Joan Sinclaire said, taking a tissue from her purse, then spreading it across her lap, "that wretched little girl's father was a taxi driver. Our family has certain standards to uphold."

"Is it true you also disapproved of Michael?"

"Don't get me started on that."

"Then you disapproved?"

"His father collected unemployment."

"I understand his father was ill."

"Our daughter was fine until she married that man. There are some things a law degree cannot repair."

Carolyn turned again to the father: "Tell me, Mr. Sinclaire, do you—"

"The appellation is *doctor*, Doctor. Ph.D.," Louis Sinclaire said.

"He's a professor of philosophy. Head of the department, I might add," said Joan.

"My apologies," said Carolyn. "Tell me, Professor, have you felt it necessary to 'guide,' as you say, your children in areas other than selecting and approving their friends?"

He took several broad steps about the room, then leaned against Carolyn's desk. "The responsibility of parenting is great," he said, as he switched an empty pipe from one corner of his mouth to the other. "The educating, the molding, the building of minds." He bent forward, pressing toward Carolyn. " 'Give me four years to teach the children and the seed I have sown will never be uprooted.' Socrates." He stood back, stuffing tobacco into his pipe.

"I believe the phrase was Lenin's." Carolyn leaned forward with a match.

"Uh, yes. Lenin. Yes, I believe Lenin has been credited with that."

"What Louis is trying to say . . ." Joan touched the small, neat twist of hair at the nape of her neck, "is that we have often used a gentle hand in directing. A child cannot know what is best for his or her life."

"It seems that's still the problem," Carolyn said. "Talia the woman, like Talia the child, is unable to make decisions; to know what she wants. Her starvation, started as a means of self-control, has become a means to gain your attention. That's one of the things we need to establish: why has Talia found it necessary to go to such measures to arouse sympathy and attention?"

"That child has had every moment of our attention. The idea is nonsense."

"Mrs. Sinclaire, one of Talia's main complaints is that she is not listened to."

"I refuse to be scapegoated for an inane illness that in our daughter's case does not apply." She rose from her chair. "Louis? Are you coming?"

He stared at the row of diplomas and certificates lined on one of Carolyn's walls.

"Let me read you both something." Carolyn retrieved two folded sheets of paper from Talia's file. "I asked that Talia write how she feels about herself and her illness. I think you should hear this before you decide to leave." She unfolded the paper and read the minute, closely spaced lettering which leaned acutely to the left.

" 'How do I feel about myself? Do you know the poem by Emily Dickinson, Doctor? *Safe in their Alabaster Chambers—Untouched by Morning—And untouched by Noon*—I often feel that way about myself and my illness;—*the meek member of the Resurrection*—hidden within a netherworld, alone and unaffecting. I am able to see those around me, but I cannot touch them, they are out there in reality, out of reach. I often want to call to them, those on the outside, but even if they were to hear me, even if they were to listen, what would I say?

" 'Before, when younger, I had nothing. Now I have the illness. I know it isn't a solution, but it's something I can no longer stop. It is my only pride. If I were to stop I feel I would lose everything; slip away; lost without anyone knowing;—*Soundless as a dot—on a Disc of Snow*—

" 'You asked me why I must keep moving. No answer, except that when I halt a terrible cloud comes over me, engulfing me with guilt. It follows me always—this ominous vapor—it knows no death. The question of eating? There is no question; it is the answer. My existence. I think of nothing now, save food, its origin and its end. Food is dread and food is joy. When I eat one bite, it is pleasure immediately turned to guilt and something I must quickly rid myself of.

" 'You tell me there is hope; that I can get better. I want to believe you, but I can't. It is pride, as you say, pride that cannot be stopped. If you have only one thing you hold on to it. You don't, you can't, let go. I would like to believe I'll be better, but I feel quite certain I will not.' "

Carolyn refolded the papers and returned them to the file. "Talia is searching for autonomy, and the only way she thinks she can obtain it is to have complete mastery over her body. She is protected with her illness; it has become an obsession with her, her only pride."

"She has always been dramatic," said Joan.

"Mrs. Sinclaire, your daughter is very ill. She needs your help."

Joan opened her handbag and removed a cigarette. She lit it with a quavering hand and quickly inhaled.

"Joan, what are you doing?"

"Smoking, Louis."

"You don't smoke!"

"There are a few things, Louis, you do not know." She inhaled again, deeply, and turned to Carolyn. "Dr. Stepler, you are probably not aware that our daughter did not have this *illness* until she married. It is obviously Michael who is to blame."

"In nearly all cases of anorexia nervosa, patients do not begin obsessive dieting until they have an initial break with the family. Usually a trip to summer camp or their first semester at college. In Talia's case, the separation came with marriage. The underlying problems have been there for years."

"She was a happy child. Everyone in our community said so. You can go to Athens today and they still talk about 'that raven-haired Sinclaire child.' Tell her, Louis!"

"She seemed happy." He sat forward in the chair, the pipe, unlit, held in his hands between his knees.

"Dr. Sinclaire, you decided what Talia should study in college. Why did you insist she study English?"

"That's what she wanted," Joan Sinclaire said for her husband.

"Talia says she wanted to study art."

"She did not. She knew she shouldn't. She didn't have the eye."

"Talia says you're an artist yourself, Mrs. Sinclaire. She says you're quite good."

"There are those who said I could have been great."

"You could have been?"

"I haven't painted in some time. Not seriously."

"Why is that?"

"One relinquishes a great deal when one becomes wife and mother."

"I told her to paint. I've tried for years to get her to start again." Louis Sinclaire stood.

"Certainly! As long as it didn't interfere with your dinner being on the table and the children learning their Latin. I gave up my entire career."

"No one forced you, Joan."

"Oh, yes they did!" She turned from her husband to Carolyn. "You see, in my day, young women were not given the opportunity my daughter has had. My parents believed a woman should be educated and then that education should be allowed to rot. One was expected to marry and immediately have a child."

"Do you have anything to tie you down now, Mrs. Sinclaire? Could you go back to your painting?"

"I've been telling her to do that."

"Yes, you can all say it now, after I've thrown it away, wasted my life."

"You need to have interests of your own," Carolyn said. "You need to return to your painting as much for Talia's sake as for your own."

"Do you comprehend what she's saying, Louis? She's saying it's our fault."

"What I'm saying is that you need to try to keep from interfering with Talia's decisions. For her to establish a sense of autonomy you need to stop telling her what she should do with her life; what foods she should eat; what clothes to wear. And it would help if you developed your own interests. It might even be wise for you to have counseling yourself."

"I don't beleive this! Louis, have you heard what she's said?"

"I heard her, Joan."

"And Dr. Sinclaire, it would be helpful if you began trying to have a more open relationship with Talia. If you try to be more affectionate and truly listen to your daughter. Don't answer her questions with some intellectual riposte. Talia needs to know you are honestly listening; that you care."

"He has always listened to that child. Everyone knows we spent hours in family conversation when the children were growing up."

"You keep referring to Talia as 'that child,' or 'our daughter.' She has a name; use it. And from now on I want you to speak of yourselves as 'we' or 'I.' Don't put everything under the terms of how 'the community' or 'our friends' regarded your family."

Joan took another cigarette and lit it, lips compressed.

"How long have you been doing that?" Dr. Sinclaire watched his wife.

"For twenty-five years." She inhaled and blew smoke his way. "My husband comes from a long line of Methodist ministers, Dr. Stepler. Of course he became agnostic when he went to Harvard, but he's still as puritanical as his father. Care for a smoke, Louis?"

The man sank against a window sill, his back pressed against glass.

"It would help Talia, as well as yourselves, if you began counseling immediately. Have you ever sought professional help with your marriage?"

"A union does not endure for over thirty years if it is flawed. The only problem is our daughter's illness. There has never been anything wrong until now. Louis will support me in that." She looked to her husband.

"Talia has felt guilty for years because of the demands a family has put on you, Mrs. Sinclaire. Because of your lost career."

"I have never implied such a thing."

"Yes, you have." Louis Sinclaire walked to his wife. "Joan, you've said it to us all."

"I am being accused."

"No one is accusing," Carolyn said. "We're only trying to establish what has made Talia go to such dangerous measures."

"I will not be vilified."

The telephone on Carolyn's desk rang; she answered the call, then returned to the Sinclaires. "Talia is outside," she said. "In a moment I'm going to ask her to join us. I think it'll be helpful to engage in a joint session for a while."

Joan grabbed her purse. "You may have your session without me."

"Mrs. Sinclaire, you, especially, need to be here."

"I will not be further persecuted in front of my daughter. Louis, we're going home."

"No, Joan, we're not. We're going to stay here and listen to what this woman has to say. We owe Talia that much."

Talia stood, her back to her parents and Carolyn.

"Talia, let's talk about your family," Carolyn said. "Do you feel you have a place within the family?"

"She doesn't want to answer. She realizes the absurdity of this," said Joan Sinclaire. "We should all go home."

Carolyn continued: "Talia, do you remember what we talked about the last time we were together? You said you were jealous of Allyson and you felt guilty because of that."

"An absolute prevarication. She was never jealous of Allyson."

"Mrs Sinclaire, it would be helpful if we allow Talia to talk. Now, Talia, do you remember what you said?"

Talia walked to the window. She traced a finger along the sill.

"Talia, there's no reason to be afraid. You may say what you feel."

"She's not afraid. We're her parents," said Joan.

"Talia, tell us how you felt when Allyson died. Do you remember what you said about being overwhelmed with guilt?"

"She felt no guilt. You're as bad as the other doctor, putting thoughts in her head."

"Joan, keep your damn mouth closed!" Dr. Sinclaire stared at his wife.

"Do you see what you've done? This ridiculous illness! It's ruining our lives. All that child has to do is eat and everything will be straightened out."

"That's not the answer to Talia's problems, Mrs. Sinclaire. We're going to have to work together—"

"It's her fault. We never had a moment's worry until this stupid anorexia came about."

"Mrs. Sinclaire, *please*."

"This is the thanks I get. After the years I've devoted to that child. I gave up everything for her. My talent. My career."

"I made you give up nothing, Mother!" Talia's hands were spread in front of her, palms up; her teeth were clenched. "It isn't my fault! You did it yourself! You gave it up because you were afraid. And you—" she turned to her father. "You've given me nothing but criticism. You've hidden behind your erudition and let her push us around."

Talia stalked about the room, her hands now clenched at her sides. "I'm the one who's suffering! Me! I'm the one in pain. It isn't my fault, Mother!" She stomped. "It isn't my fault!" She halted then, suddenly, finding herself in the middle of the room, alone, the others watching. She bit a trembling lip, wrapped herself in her arms and began shifting from one foot to the other. "I'm sorry," she said; it was a whisper

"This outcry is inexcusable," said Joan Sinclaire, now on her feet.

"I'm sorry, Mother."

"Of course you are."

Carolyn walked between the two women. "Talia, you don't have to be sorry. You were angry. You said what you felt."

"Leave her alone." Joan held out her hands, beckoning to Talia.

"I'm sorry, Mother." The plea was still a whisper as Talia moved with Joan. "I'm sorry, Mother. I'm *sorry*." The words were growing louder as she walked. "I'm sorry."

"Mother knows you're sorry. Mother knows." Mrs. Sinclaire regained her seat, holding her daughter's arms.

"I'm so sorry." Talia crawled into her mother's lap.

"It's all right." Joan Sinclaire stared at Carolyn while stroking Talia's hair. "It's all right," she said and began rocking the shaking bundle back and forth. "Mother has you now."

== 16 ==

"Talia, you don't have to feel guilty for what you said."

Carolyn moved closer to her patient, able to see the soft fluff of hair, characteristic of anorexics, which grew on Talia's exposed and rawboned arms. Talia wore the dress she always wore when the weather was cool; a flimsy jersey with short sleeves. And, as usual, she stood. For the past ten minutes she had faced the shelving unit which dominated the entire length of one office wall, and ignored Carolyn, running a finger along the books on Carolyn's shelves.

"Talia, you did nothing bad yesterday," Carolyn persisted. "You said what you felt."

Talia picked up one of the volumes, rubbing her hand in a caressing fashion over the book's spine. "I was taught to read before I was five," she said.

"You were angry, Talia. There's nothing wrong with that."

"Children should respect their parents." The fondling stopped.

"Yes, they should. But sometimes even parents are wrong; they can act as immature as children. You were right, Talia. Your mother's problems aren't your fault."

"Mother has no problems." Talia returned the book, then added in a barely audible susurration: "Except for me."

"Everyone has problems; even mothers." Carolyn waited a moment, watching Talia as she moved down the row of books, the indentations and protrusions of her spine visible through blue polyester, then continued: "You're always telling me you have no effect on others, that your existence doesn't matter. Talia, it does. Yesterday you made your mother angry; anxious. That may not be a pleasant effect, but Talia, it *is* an effect. You arouse feelings in others. You make a difference."

Talia had turned, staring, but then as the words stopped, she moved away.

"Mother doesn't anger. She's above that."

"Everyone angers. It's a normal emotion, and one we all should express."

"This is a Bufano, isn't it?"

"Yes, Talia, it is," Carolyn said as the stick-figure woman stroked a piece of sculpture, the focal point of Carolyn's shelves. It was carved of white Carrara marble and formed into the sleek, simple body of a bear. Carolyn had purchased it in San Francisco years ago; a graduation gift for herself when she left the University of California Medical School. The smooth, unadorned lines of the animal had become a symbol of Carolyn's free, uncomplicated life; she considered it her prototype in stone.

"I'm impressed," Carolyn said. "You're the first person, since I've been in Atlanta, to recognize that as a Bufano."

"Not even Mother?"

"No, not even your mother. See, Talia, you have many wonderful qualities for people to admire. You don't need your dieting to gain their respect."

Talia still stroked the animal's neck. "I have quite an interest in American sculpture. I should have studied—" She backed away from the shelves.

"Should have studied what, Talia? Art?"

"I only wanted to study art history. I wouldn't have touched fine art. I wouldn't have tried to take that away."

"Take what away?" Carolyn waited as Talia returned to the sculpture.

"Mother's art." Talia said, cupping a hand under the animal's long, straight head. "She wasn't even that good." Her voice was growing louder. "Her colors were weak and her perspective has always been off."

"Did you tell them what you wanted, Talia? What you wanted to study?"

"I couldn't."

"Why couldn't you?" Carolyn said.

"It would have made Father angry, the way he was with James."

"Why was your father angry with James?"

"He said James should be a professor, that he should study philosophy like Father. But James wanted to study medicine. They were always arguing about him becoming a doctor. There was always a fight."

"So to prevent your father from becoming angry, the way he did with James, you didn't go against what he wanted. Is that correct?"

"I couldn't. It would have been bad."

"Talia, it isn't *bad* to ask for something you want."

"It is."

"Do you think James was a bad person?"

"No! James was good. He was wonderful."

"But your brother was only expressing what he wanted to be, wasn't he?" Carolyn waited a moment, hoping Talia would respond. "You see, it isn't bad to do that. And it isn't wrong to resent your parents now because they made you study English."

"They made me do nothing."

"I must have misunderstood."

"Everyone knows I love literature. I read the *Iliad* three times before eighth grade. We're a cultured family, you know."

"Are you proud of that?"

Talia swung around, holding the stone creature in her arms. "They made us study when other children were at play! Allyson would cry. She'd go to the window, stomp her feet, knock on the glass, and cry."

"But you didn't did you?"

"No." A whisper.

"You did your studies and you never cried or went against your parents' wishes."

"I did everything they said. *Everything!* I was so good, Dr. Stepler. I was always so *good*—so—goddamned good." Talia's voice was tremulous now, fluctuating between tears and a whisper, as she walked to the window clutching the bear.

"Yes, you were very good," said Carolyn, slowly rescuing the sculpture from Talia's hands. "Why was it so important, Talia, to be so good; to do everything your parents said?"

"They're always right."

"Were they right to decide what you should study in college?"

"I have perfect parents."

"Was your father right to make you play tennis?"

"I hated tennis!" She walked behind Carolyn's desk. "I'd go out there and hit the ball as hard as I possibly could. I'd make it go over the fence and I'd pretend it was Father's shrunken head rolling across the lawn." She dropped into Carolyn's desk chair, the muscles around her eyes protruding as she held her face in her hands. "I'm sorry. I didn't mean it about Father."

"You don't have to apologize."

"I love my parents."

"Of course you love them. You just don't love everything they've done and said. Talia, you did things you didn't want to do, things you didn't enjoy. It's normal to feel resentful about that."

"They've given me everything."

"But did they give you the things you wanted?"

Talia jerked her legs from side to side, each time turning the large swivel chair.

"It's all right to want to do the things you enjoy," Carolyn said. "It's all right to be kind to yourself."

"I wanted to go bowling with my friend."

"Did you tell your father that?"

"Tennis is more of our family's class."

"Is that what your father said?"

"He's always right." Talia stood and moved away from Carolyn. "He has a Ph.D."

"Does your father play tennis?"

"He taught me."

"Does he play golf?"

"Father hates golf. Not enough exercise; a waste of time."

"Talia, you have the same rights your father has. You should be able to choose the activities you enjoy, not the ones someone else selects for you. And you shouldn't feel guilty for going ahead with your own wishes."

"Father has done what is best for me."

"Sometimes a person needs to decide what is best for herself."

"I've committed a sin." She had returned to a whisper.

"No, Talia, you haven't."

"I've stolen."

"What have you stolen?"

"Money."

"When did you steal money?"

"Yesterday, from Mother. And from Michael, lots of times."

"Tell me about it."

"For food. I stole it for food."

"Doesn't Michael give you money for food?"

"I can't use it for this."

"For what, Talia?"

"Candy. I had to." She was drifting into the morose monotone she often used.

"I'm listening, Talia," Carolyn said. "I want to hear."

"I took the money from Mother's wallet when she went to get the car. After they left for Athens I ran to Cloudt's and bought it. Ate it all."

"What did you eat?"

"The candy. Eight bars. Chocolate."

"And then what did you do?"

"You know."

"Tell me."

"Regurgitated."

"Why did you do it, Talia?"

"I don't know."

"Think about it. Think about what happened when you were with your mother. What made you want to get the money so you could eat?"

"It felt empty. I didn't know what to do."

"So you ate the candy?"

"Yes."

"And then why did you throw up?"

"I felt so bad; so guilty. It was wrong. And it was wrong to yell at Mother. She's a good mother. A perfect mother."

Carolyn twisted her neck, trying to remove the pain that always came when, near the end of a session with Talia, she felt they had reached nowhere. The pain shot up from the base of her skull and ended in a dreaded jab behind her eyes.

"Talia, you mustn't keep feeling guilty because of what happened yesterday. You didn't do anything wrong. You thought your father had been weak, maybe even childish and silly. And you thought your mother used you as an excuse for not having a career. Those things made you angry and you were forced to shout."

"Sinclaires do not shout."

"Your mother shouted yesterday. Do you remember? Did you hear her shout?"

"She was upset."

"Weren't you? You have the same prerogatives as Mother. You're allowed to shout. There is nothing bad about that."

The jabs behind Carolyn's pupils continued, penetrating through her head. She sat for a few silent moments, watching as her patient paced near the door. Talia's weight had vacillated since their therapy began, never reaching more than eighty pounds. It was now less than seventy, lower than it had ever been. The gorging and vomiting, instead of decreasing, seemed to be getting worse. And each time Carolyn felt they were progressing, Talia's guilt and stubborn self-accusation oscillated to the extreme.

"Talia, when you came for the first session, I told

you there must be an increase in your weight. But instead of gaining, you've lost."

The pacing stopped. "I count them in minuses," Talia said. "In the back of my brain I have this little corner where I'm stacking up negative pounds."

"In your letter you told me you wanted to get well."

"Yes."

"Then you must gain weight, Talia. You're at a very low nutritional level. You and I cannot work on your psychological problems when you're being affected by an undernourished body. Do you understand?"

"One has to whip one's body into control. Make it one's slave. See?" She pulled up her dress, exposing an abdomen pressed against spine, and panties which hung from protruding hipbones. "I say, 'Acquiesce, body!' and body does. I am at the helm."

"I've talked with a nutritionist and worked out a diet for you. You don't have to worry about gaining too much; about getting fat. This will only help you reach and maintain a healthy balance."

"It's rather like brainwashing," Talia said. "If you tell the body it isn't hungry enough times, then it isn't."

"Talia, are you listening to me?"

Silence.

"We aren't going to be able to help you until you at least begin to eat," Carolyn said. "Talia, people don't love you because you're thin; because you can withstand the pain and hunger of starving yourself. They love you because you're you."

"This is me. It's all I am."

"Talia," Carolyn spoke slowly, so there would be no mistake as to the weight and meaning of her words, "if you don't gain weight in the next week, you'll have to be hospitalized. Fed intravenously."

"Go ahead, do it!" Talia stood with the hem of her dress still held high, proudly displaying withered legs and protruding bones. "The tubes can't feed me if I tell my body not to accept."

"Talia, do you really want to do that? Go to the hospital and leave Michael?"

"He doesn't care."

"Why do you say that?"

"He doesn't."

"You're a very special person. He must love you very much."

"He has someone else."

Carolyn sat forward.

"There's someone he goes to. At night. He calls her on the phone."

Damn it! how could he have been so careless? "You seem quite sure," Carolyn said.

"I've known for a long time."

"It's easy to be mistaken about things like that. You could be wrong."

"You know I'm not wrong."

"How could I know such a thing, Talia?"

"Because I told you!" She moved across the room, returning to the bear. "A fine piece of sculpture," she said.

"Talia," Carolyn lingered over the name, giving herself time to think of the proper thing to say. "Michael wants very much for you to get well."

"It doesn't matter."

"Yes it does. It matters very much. If not for Michael then for yourself. Talia, we need to start working on those positive pounds." Carolyn grabbed a sheet of bond paper from her desk and quickly scrawled the number 80 across the sheet. "Talia, we'll start with this number; eighty pounds will be the first goal." She tacked the paper to the wall over her desk. "Talia, do this for yourself. Not for Michael or Mother or anyone but yourself."

Talia stared at the Bufano.

"Talia, you must."

"I told you, it doesn't matter."

Carolyn answered the phone on the first ring, the loud knell one last irritation of the day. She glanced at her watch; nearly seven. She was exhausted, headachy, ready to go. "Yes? This is Dr. Stepler," she said, her voice acidic.

"Carolyn, this is Michael."

Blood surged to her temple, fuel to the explosion already within her head.

"Hello, Mike."

He cleared his throat, then asked: "Did you see her today?"

Speak her name, damn it! she thought. Don't any of you ever speak her name? "Yes," she said sharply, "I saw Talia."

"How's she doing?"

"I don't know."

"What do you mean, you don't know? I'm holding in my hand a bill for eight hundred and fifty dollars and you tell me you don't know how she's doing?"

"You were aware of my fees before therapy with Talia began."

"Well, sure. But I rather assumed our previous relationship would alter that some."

"You assumed wrong!" Carolyn held a pencil, pressing it between thumb and fingers, wanting to break it in half.

Mike cleared his throat again, fracturing the silence, and spoke: "I suppose you'll be flying to Washington for the seminar on terrorism?" His voice sounded restrained.

"I won't be working on that. My retainer with Coastal is up in a couple of weeks and I don't plan to renew."

"Why not? I thought the money was great."

"My practice has grown. I haven't the time anymore." A pause. "Mike, if there isn't anything else, I need to go."

"I thought maybe we could get together for a drink. To discuss Talia. I could pick you up."

"I'll be glad to discuss Talia, in fact I think we should, but not tonight: not over a drink."

"Over coffee, then. I'd really like to talk."

"Phone my secretary Monday morning. She'll arrange an appointment."

"Carolyn, her parents are complaining. Jumping down my neck. Joan thinks you're making her worse; that you're doing it all wrong."

"I know that."

"Well, what the hell am I supposed to do?"

"You're supposed to hang on. Keep fighting for her. And stop calling me."

"Is she getting any better? Is there any change?"

"It's going to take time."

"Carolyn, have coffee with me. Just this once. I swear I won't ask again."

"No."

"Carolyn, I need to talk."

"Then talk to Talia, damn it. She needs you now."

=== 17 ===

Carolyn lay fetal on the sofa, awakened by the simultaneous sound of stereo needle scratching the heart of Dvořák and timer from the oven buzzing on the stove. She pulled herself free of an afghan, which had crawled up her body and worked its way around her neck, and remembered that while she slept, she had dreamt of mice. Three blind ones.

One blew syncopated smoke signals into the air while another, bespectacled, pretended he could see. And a third wore a hairless chignon formed by its tail.

Carolyn rose from the sofa, lifted stereo arm and needle, turned *New World Symphony* to the opposite side, and walked to the kitchen at pace with the largo from Symphony No. 5.

The dream had been a hideous one, with Carolyn being bound and tied by the mice, tickled by their whiskers, and guffawed at by their wide, incisor-filled mouths. They built nests in her hair, tunneled through her clothing, and with little rodent feet ran up and down her spine. That she rarely remembered having dreamt made the fantasy more vivid and even more absurd.

She opened the oven door, warming herself, shaking herself free of the dream, and pulled an aluminum tray from the oven rack. Steam escaped, clouding the air, as she lifted foil from the tray. It was the last of her inventory of frozen dinners: dry enchiladas and tasteless grains of rice. Not hungry, she set a place for herself at the kitchen table; her Saturday lunch. The fact was, she needed to eat. She had lost five or six pounds over the last few weeks and it had begun to show in her face and in the fit of her clothes. The loss was unintentional; she had simply forgotten to eat. For her, meals had always been a thing one did alone; a quick sandwich over books or packaged dinners in front of the TV while she had waited for her mother to come home. The consumption of food was entirely pragmatic—a means of energy and sustainment for a highly efficient and intricate machine. She drank milk and water liberally, salted food sparingly, and tried to provide herself with one hot meal a day; all with the same enthusiasm she had for changing the oil, requesting a lube job, or refueling her car. Maintenance. Nothing more.

She took two bites of the bland, packaged food and washed it down with a swallow of milk. There was irony in this, that she gave no thought to eating, did it merely to survive, while Talia tortured herself with visions of food and yet maintained a near-skeletal appearance and weight of just barely seventy pounds. Talia insisted she was never hungry, but Carolyn knew the pain she endured was extreme. Patients who had recovered from anorexia described the details of their self-imposed starvation with horror. Yet, the more weight they had lost—the more rigid the standards these patients had set for themselves, the more acute their agony—the prouder they had become of their masterful feat and bizarre obsessions. Each day Talia became more delighted with her scarecrow body; she flaunted her ultrathinness, professing her weight was "fine."

Carolyn pushed away the food, half-eaten. She was worried. She had stayed at her office until eleven o'clock last night, going through Talia's file again, searching for something in that volume of personal history that would be helpful in treating Talia.

Carolyn was dumping the remains of her lunch down the disposal when the doorbell rang. At two o'clock on a Saturday afternoon she expected no one. This was a day she spent on herself; napping if she wanted, running errands she didn't have time for during the week. And there was no one in her life right now, not even friends, who might drop by. She had taken a position of semiseclusion over the last several weeks, seeing virtually no one except colleagues; fellow psychiatrists or physicans for lunch. She had accepted one date since the split with Mike; a designer she had met at a party during Christmas. He took her to a dark little bistro in Buckhead, talked parapsychology, and wore a silk shirt with fagoting around the sleeves. The evening had been unrewarding in every conceivable way.

She finished at the sink, turned the stereo off in the living room, and walked to the door. Mike stood at the top of the stairs, unshaven, his hair peculiarly ratty and blown.

"May I come in?" He removed a hand from his pocket and rubbed it across his face.

"I'm expecting guests," she lied, and started to close the door.

"Carolyn, please." He pushed his way inside. "Give me a couple of minutes."

"I'm busy."

"I need to talk to you. Carolyn, *please*. I won't stay long."

"*Look*, I don't want you here."

"Two minutes, Carolyn. It's about Talia."

"Listen, Mike, I don't want you here. Talia knows you had an affair."

"How do you know that?"

"I'm her therapist, remember?"

"She knows?" He slumped down on the sofa. "What did she say?"

"Come to my office Monday and we'll discuss it." She remained at the door.

"I never meant for her to find out."

"No one ever does."

"She's not getting any better, is she?"

"There's been some improvement."

"But not much, right?"

"Mike, go home."

"I can't. Her parents are there; been there since seven this morning."

"Damn it, that's part of the problem." Carolyn took a seat on the far side of the couch. "What do they want?"

"Talia told them you said something about going to the hospital. Joan would rather die."

"The woman needs help. Counseling," Carolyn said.

"She's hysterical, trying to get Talia to eat. They've been at it all day."

"Did you tell her to leave?"

"I didn't tell her anything. I didn't have a chance. Carolyn, I've never seen anything like what's going on over there. I've never seen Talia this way."

"What way? What's she doing?"

"Joan came barging in with her arms full of groceries, saying no daughter of hers was going to a psychiatric ward, that all Talia needed was food. She started throwing pots and pans around, opening cans of soup. At first Talia just watched, like she normally does. Then all off a sudden—I don't know—she kind of went crazy."

"Crazy, how?"

"She told Joan to get the hell out of her kitchen, that no one was going to make her eat. Joan started pouring soup, spreading butter on bread, saying that Talia wasn't going to embarrass them all. Kept saying how Talia was a disgrace and she was ruining the family. And all Talia kept saying was, 'Good! Good!' "

Carolyn moved from the sofa and poured Mike a glass of wine. She handed him the burgundy. "Go on, Mike. What happened next?"

He tilted the goblet to one side and then the other, watching the red wine form wet sheets against the glass.

"Mike? Is that all?"

He placed the goblet on the table, without having touched the wine. "Joan—she, uh, started saying how she wasn't going to leave until Talia had eaten. And

Talia said it was fine with her, Joan could stay all day if she liked, but no one was going to make her eat. It was her body—the same crap she's been saying for months. Then Joan came back with some remark about how disgusting Talia looked, how skinny. When she said that, Talia unbuttoned her robe, and she stood there, in the middle of the kitchen, nude. In front of her father; all of us. She just stood there. Smiling. Grinning actually, saying how her body was fine, perfectly fine. Joan screamed—I thought she was going to faint—and Dr. Sinclare left the room. He hadn't said anything all day; just watched, looking kind of sad."

"Drink the wine. It'll make you feel better."

"That grin; it was so crazy. I mean, she seemed to enjoy it so much."

"She enjoys the attention, Mike."

"Joan started trying again to get her to eat. Started pleading. Then Talia took a jar of vinegar out of a cabinet, poured half the bottle into a glass and drank it. The whole thing."

Carolyn nodded.

"You act as if that were normal. It's not normal. It's strange. Sick. Carolyn, she drank straight vinegar."

"No, it's not normal, but it *is* characteristic of anorexics. They like their meager amounts of food to be as spicy, as acidic as possible. Mustard, pepper, horseradish. Anything with a strong, pungent taste. She probably took a diuretic afterward."

"I don't know what she did. I left with Joan crying about how it was everyone's fault. Yours. Mine. The professor's. I don't know," he emptied half the wine with one swallow. "Maybe it is."

"It's no one person's fault."

"And now she knows I had an affair. I didn't mean for her to find out. I thought I was careful."

"I know that."

"Maybe I did cause all this. She was fine before we married."

"Stop it, Mike. You know it isn't your fault."

"I don't know that. I was rough on her before I knew she was ill. I did some cruel things."

"You were angry; because she wasn't being a wife. But whatever you did, it didn't cause the dysfunction. The problems have been there for years."

He opened his mouth and a spectrum of color appeared momentarily on a sheath of saliva which quickly dissolved. "I'm scared," he said.

"She's going to be all right."

It had begun to rain. Wind blew through a window, ballooning the drapes.

"I guess I should go," he said.

Carolyn took his hand and spoke as she might to any patient needing her help: "You may stay if you like."

Mike walked from the bedroom, fastening his pants. "Why didn't you wake me?" he said.

"You needed the rest."

"I can't believe I fell asleep. What time is it?"

Carolyn looked at her watch. "Quarter to seven."

"Jesus, I've got to go."

"Before you do, I'd like to discuss something."

He sat on the sofa tying his shoes.

"I think Talia should be hospitalized, Mike."

"She won't go."

"I think she will. Anorexics generally like all the attention and sympathy their illness brings. She may resist at first, but she'll go. I think she must go."

"Her mother's not going to like it."

"No, I don't imagine she will. But I'm going to ask that Mrs. Sinclaire stay away, at least until Talia has reached a safe level of weight, hopefully ninety pounds. Right now her weight's so low it affects her mental state. It affects me too. I can't treat her properly when I'm constantly anxious about her physical well-being."

"If it's that bad I don't understand why you've waited so long."

"Most hospitals don't have the experienced personnel or the facilities to cope with the demands of an anorexic. But Talia's situation has become critical. She must gain weight and if she's not going to do it herself then it must be done intravenously."

"What do you want me to do?"

"Take her to Piedmont Hospital tomorrow. I called Dr. Lambdin while you were asleep. He and I see eye to eye on this."

"I was supposed to go out of town tomorrow."

"Can you postpone it?"

"I don't know. It's about the merger. Everything's hanging in the balance."

"For Talia too. If you can't change your plans, call me. Otherwise, Dr. Lambdin and I'll be there to admit her tomorrow afternoon at three. And Mike, I know this is going to be difficult, but you need to keep her parents away."

With Mike gone, Carolyn went to the small study in her second bedroom. She opened the file she had brought from her office last night, and removed the two snapshots whose difference Talia had not been able to discern. Carolyn's thoughts were with Mike as she studied the photograph which was torn in half; the one showing Talia holding the hand of a missing person. The hand was his. The effects of anorexia nervosa were devastating, she knew, not only to the patient but also to each family member. And as she examined the hand which grasped Talia's, Carolyn realized Mike probably was being affected more than anyone else involved. The Sinclaires, in their own pathetic way, had each other. And Talia had all of them in a sense. But Mike had no one right now. As in the snapshot, he seemed torn from the others; alone.

She picked up the second photograph; Talia: the angry, stalking figure. Carolyn knew now Talia was more ill even than she had first believed. The condition had gone too far; the starvation had ramifications beyond mere emancipation. Talia had become dehydrated; the weight loss could affect the circulatory system and disturb the electrolyte balance.

Carolyn studied the photograph, wanting to reach out to Talia and shake her to reality. She, the physician, was now concerned more with the physiological aspects of her patient's pitiable state than with the psychological. She was literally fighting for this woman's life.

18

Carolyn had stood for some minutes watching—the back of Talia's head bent over, her hands gripping wheelchair arms—after Talia had been admitted and wheelchaired down the hospital corridor. She had seemed to Carolyn then the portrait of a geriatric woman, angry but resigned to a nemesis of ill fate.

It had taken over an hour to get Talia admitted, fill out hospital and insurance forms, and finally arrive at her designated room. In that hour, surrounded by family, doctors, and hospital personnel, Talia had spoken tersely or not at all.

But for the last fifteen minutes, alone in the room with Carolyn, she had talked incessantly, complaining of the room and the appearance of nurses, and ridiculing Dr. Lambdin. She sat propped against pillows, torso upright, emaciated arms lapped over her chest. Two parallel ripples in the sheet revealed the slightness of her legs and how far apart they seemed set at the hips.

"Who asked him here, anyway?" Talia said. The ripples grew into arches, tenting the sheet.

"I did." Carolyn walked to one side of the bed. "Dr. Lambdin is going to handle the programming of your weight and intravenous intake."

"I don't need him. I don't want him here."

"With his help you won't feel so tired and weak all the time."

"I'm not weak and I don't want him touching me." She sat taller in the bed, sliding her feet toward her, elevating the tent. "And I'm not going to eat!"

174

"No one's going to force you."

"I don't want him bothering me."

"He's here to help you. He wants you well."

"He wants me fat."

"Talia, you're not going to get fat. Dr. Lambdin is going to provide you with a good diet so that won't happen. I promise you, he won't let you gain too much, too fast."

"We don't have the money for this sort of thing."

"Your husband has insurance, Talia." Carolyn walked between the window and bed. "How do you feel?"

"I feel like this!" She poked a finger at her arms and face.

"Are you comfortable?"

"And I don't want those dull-witted nurses bothering me."

"They have to do their job."

"They won't make me eat. Nobody's going to make me fat."

"You're right; no one will. We aren't going to let you gain too much."

"I don't need to gain at *all*." She crawled to a kneeling position on the bed. "See!"

Carolyn turned away and stared out the window. "Talia, this business of not eating isn't the real problem. I think you know that."

As Carolyn moved back to the bed Talia sank against the pillows, her head a tight ball precariously pivoted upon a spindle of a neck; her arms stiff right angles at her sides.

"While you're here you can relax, Talia. You won't have to feel guilty for getting rest. You'll be doing it for me."

"I don't care anything about you."

"Then care about yourself."

"My mother thinks I shouldn't be here."

"Your mother isn't always right."

"Tell *her* that, why don't you?"

"Are you afraid to tell her?"

Talia pulled the cover sheet close to her neck, then began folding it neatly over her lap. "I don't want those nurses in my room."

"Avoiding the questions isn't going to help, you know."

"I'm not going to put any food in my mouth."

"Okay."

"And I'll pull the tubes out when I'm alone."

"Talia, we aren't going to get anywhere until you *co-operate*. Until you've gained weight. Now, I've told you we won't let you gain too much; you're going to have to trust me. I can't do a good job of helping you if I'm constantly worried about your health this way."

"You're concerned?"

"Of course I'm concerned. Very."

"Because I'm your patient."

"Because you're you. I care about you, Talia."

"You care about no one."

"Talia, I think you know that's not true."

"Yes, it is. I've watched you; I see you as you are."

"How am I?"

"Afraid of getting too close."

Carolyn picked up her purse and fit the strap over her shoulder. "It's getting late."

"Sometimes I think your chamber's more protective than mine."

"Good night, Talia. I'll see you tomorrow."

"See! You're more of a coward than I."

The hospital lounge was an institutional green. Talia's parents sat at opposite sides of a low wooden bench inside the room. Mike stood alone, leaning against a far wall, staring out a large window which overlooked Peachtree Street. He was so far from the others that Carolyn wondered if he was aware of what was being said.

"I'm not going to interfere. I merely want to see her," Joan Sinclaire said, twisting a Kleenex; the polish was chipped on her nails.

"Seeing her would interfere," said Carolyn.

"If I had her home one week we could make everything right. Things would be the way they're supposed to be."

"Anorexics like to have their abnegating actions perceived as very special, Mrs. Sinclaire. In the hospital that won't happen. The nurses have been forewarned. They know how to react to Talia's demands."

"I know how to react. In one week I could have her eating. I know what to do. She'd be well."

"Joan, I don't think that's what Dr. Stepler's saying." Louis Sinclaire moved down the bench, sliding nearer his wife.

"Why are you always in agreement with her? Don't you care?"

"*Joan.*"

"Why is everyone on her side?"

"Mrs. Sinclaire, getting Talia to eat isn't the answer to her problem."

"Then why is she here?"

"Because her condition has become critical. Your daughter's weight has now dropped to sixty-nine pounds. If we don't act quickly Talia could suffer physical consequences which will affect her the rest of her life. Or the situation could become beyond redemption."

"Do you mean fatal? Are you trying to scare me?"

"Mrs. Sinclaire, at the moment *I'm* scared."

"I want Talia to come home."

Carolyn moved to Joan's side of the room and sat on a small table in front of the bench. "I realize that you love your daughter, and that's the reason you want her home. But since you do love her, you're going to have to give her up."

"All she has to do is gain weight."

"But she's not going to do that without intravenous assistance."

The woman looked away from Carolyn. She began furiously scraping the polish on her nails.

"Mrs. Sinclaire, do you know what happens to people who starve? Who go for months and years without nutrients and food?" Carolyn waited a moment, then continued, moving closer. "They begin to suffer from protein and vitamin deficiencies. Loss of vitamin A can lead to softening or dissolution of the cornea; or the eye may become excessively dry. If the condition is prolonged, damage may be irreversible, the cornea may become enlarged or forever misshapen. And severe deficiency of vitamin A may result in tissue damage to the respiratory tract.

"With the kind of excessive vomiting and laxatives Talia has used to accelerate starvation, she could suffer from hypokalemia, a lack of potassium in the blood. This can lead to extreme changes in renal and circulatory systems; the kidneys may soon cease to function at all. Or the vomiting and malnutrition could lead to tetany, a painful condition of intermittent muscular spasms. We've already seen indications of this.

"If the body becomes too depleted of fluids and the electrolyte balance is seriously disturbed, then abnormal amounts of calcium salts may be deposited in tissue. This can cause extreme damage throughout the body, including renal and cardiac failure.

"Mrs. Sinclaire, if treatment of starving patients is delayed, not only may they suffer physical damage the rest of their lives, they're dangerously vulnerable to acute infection."

The only sounds were from traffic outside and from Mike repeatedly cracking the knuckles on each hand.

"We don't want this to happen to Talia, Mrs. Sinclaire. Her speech could be impaired. It could become difficult or impossible to walk. She could become an invalid. And I must tell you the condition could be terminal."

Louis Sinclaire took his wife's hand. "There won't be any trouble from us, Doctor."

"How long?" Joan said. "How long before I can see my child?"

"That depends on Talia. If she's receptive, she could gain weight fairly rapidly. She'll be fed intravenously and given liquid protein until the act of eating solid food isn't so offensive and frightening to her. And when she does begin to eat, we'll provide her with preselected, well balanced meals so she won't be faced with decisions. As soon as a certain amount of weight has been gained, I think she'll be more relaxed; not so hostile."

"Then she can come home?"

"Possibly. If she realizes and maintains a safe weight."

"And then she'll be well."

"Hopefully she'll be on the *way* to being well. If she'll start opening up in therapy and trying to reach the root of her problems. But Mrs. Sinclaire, you're going to have to stay away for these next few weeks. Everyone involved is going to have to be very mature. In everything we do, we must think of Talia first."

Mike walked Carolyn to her car. Streetlights came on as they reached the automobile, making buzzing sounds, and awakening drops of oil in parking-lot puddles left from yesterday's rain.

"I hate to leave her like this," he said. "I don't want her to be all alone."

"Someone'll be with her around the clock and I'll see her every day. I almost think it's best you'll be gone. She needs the time without you, any of you, with no pressures or interferences."

Carolyn watched Mike as he watched a young black couple and small child standing under one of the lights. The couple swung the child by the arms, letting his tiny feet glide safely over a water-filled pothole in the tarmac. Secure, the child laughed freely and unintimidated.

"Sometimes," Mike said, watching the three, "I get angry, Carolyn. Honest-to-God mad. I mean, my folks didn't have anything, you know? My dad was sick as long as I can remember and I had to work for everything I got. But Talia wanted for nothing. I mean, I don't understand it, she's always had so much."

"Too much, maybe. That's part of the problem. In return for all she received, she felt brilliant things were expected of her. Things she was afraid she couldn't accomplish. So she began regimenting herself to be the best until the regimentation became extreme."

"I don't know," he said. "Maybe it's because of her mother. The woman's nuts."

"It would be easy to throw the blame on her, but I don't think we can. Not really. It's a combination of a lot of things. Both parents; even their parents and their parents' parents; society; Talia herself. The problem's Gordian. I don't think there's any clearcut yes or no answer."

He opened the car door for her, and after she was seated, lingered with the door still open, pushing down and pulling up on the lock.

"Carolyn, I feel so much on the outside, as if there's nothing I can do. I don't know what to say to her. I can't even touch her. I'm afraid if I go near her, she'll break. I know it sounds ridiculous, but I'm scared of her in a way."

"It isn't ridiculous," Carolyn said, rolling down the window. "I think it's fairly normal under the circumstances." She waited for a moment, while he held tight to the frame, then started the engine. "When will you be back?" she said.

"Four days. Five at the most. I wouldn't go if I didn't have to."

"I realize that."

"I don't think she does."

"She will. Give her time."

"I could come back without a job—if this merger goes through." He leaned down and grinned. "*Then* do I get a discount?"

"Credit," Carolyn said, and they both laughed. It started slowly, unsure, then expanded, one strengthened by the other until it was full and purifying in its mutuality.

He closed the door for her and pressed down the lock.

"Mike, where can I reach you—if there are any problems—if I need you to come home?"

"What kind of problems?"

"She's dehydrated. The vomiting's led to severe loss of body fluids and electrolytes. And she's so weak she can hardly stand. The next few days are critical. Everything will depend on how Talia reacts, and then, even if she regains her strength, it's only the first step."

19

The room had the musty kind of odor which comes from elderly people with scaly, unwashed scalps; from people who aid themselves in that eventual process of decay. It was dark, except for a green light which tacitly winked from the face of an IVAC machine; a watchful eye which monitored the flow to Talia's arm. Her head rested on the pillowless upper line of an obtuse angle, her body bending at the vertex of the bed. "Did they tell you?" she said, her voice sounding weaker than it had the day before.

"Tell me what?" Carolyn said it absently, knowing, as she thumbed through Talia's chart.

"About this—the *machine*."

"Isn't it working?"

"I tricked them," Talia said, baring her teeth.

"I see," and Carolyn turned a piece of paper over the lip of a metal board, continuing to read.

"Well, aren't you angry?"

"Is that what you want me to be?"

"They're so stupid," Talia said, readjusting the angle of the bed. "I watched how they did it, how they disconnected the tube, and how they pushed this button," she pointed to the green eye, "so the beeping would stop. I held my wrist under the sheet, like this," she covered her arm, "and I pumped it into a bedpan for over an hour. They didn't even know."

"Your temperature's risen," Carolyn said casually. "Almost normal. That's a good sign."

"I could do it again, if I wanted."

"Yes, I suppose you could."

"No one could stop me."

Carolyn turned from the bed and walked to the window. "Who sent the flowers? They're beautiful," she said.

"I don't want them. I don't need anything from him."

"From whom?"

"Whom do you think?"

"Michael?" Carolyn said, but Talia only stared ahead. "Why wouldn't you want the flowers, Talia?"

"If he was so worried he wouldn't send flowers. He'd be here, wouldn't he?"

"Michael didn't want to leave. He would have stayed if I had thought it was necessary. I told him to go."

"He'll be sorry."

"Is that why you won't talk to him when he phones? So he'll be sorry?"

"He tells you everything, doesn't he?"

"Michael's very concerned about you, Talia. When you wouldn't talk to him he was afraid something was wrong."

"I don't have to talk with anyone."

"No, you don't. But punishing him isn't going to help."

"Punish *him*? Look at me! Michael isn't the one who's suffering."

"You don't have to suffer either. That's what I've been trying to tell you." Carolyn sat at the edge of the bed and Talia slid her legs to the far side.

"They told you, didn't they? About the machine."

"Yes, they told me."

"I could do it again, if I wanted."

"That's true."

"Well, I don't want to," and she clicked off the lamp over her bed and closed her eyes.

"Talia, if you give this a chance, if you try to relax and get some nourishment, you're going to feel better."

"I don't want to feel better. I mean—I feel fine."

"Do you?"

"Leave me alone." She rolled to her side so Carolyn could no longer see her face.

"We could make this less difficult, if you wanted." Carolyn walked around the bed so she could watch Talia's expressions. "We could give you liquid protein and you coud do without the tubes."

"I don't want it less difficult," Talia said. "I want things to *be* difficult, don't you understand?" She kicked the sheet off her legs, the faded hospital gown hanging from her frame. "And I don't have to do what anyone says." She was shouting now. "I don't have to listen to those nurses or to you!"

"Talia, we can't help you unless you let us."

"I don't need your help; any of it!" and she tore the tube from her wrist. Blood began covering the gauze which had held the tube in place.

"*Oh, Talia . . .*"

"It didn't hurt."

"Well, I should think it would hurt a great deal," Carolyn said, appearing calm as she bandaged the bleeding arm.

"It could," Talia said, almost arrogantly, "if I let it."

"But you don't?"

"I'm not going to eat."

"All right, Talia. All right." Carolyn wheeled the IVAC around the bed and inserted the tube in the uninjured arm. "Don't eat. We'll do it this way as long as you want."

Talia stood at the tall, uncurtained windows of her room, the sunlight pouring over her profile, each ray becoming brighter as it struck the red threads of her robe. She turned as Carolyn entered the room, her body now eclipsing the sun, and pushed the IVAC machine toward the bed. She had refused to speak to anyone during the last two days, and Carolyn had finally achieved a form of communication by using handwritten notes.

"How are you feeling today?" Carolyn wrote and pressed the sheet of paper to Talia.

Talia nodded once, meaning "fine."

"Do you want anything?"

"Not hungry!" Talia sent back in her angry scrawl and then ignored Carolyn by picking up a yellow legal pad from the table by her bed.

"What are you working on?" Carolyn wrote.

Talia shrugged.

"May I see it?"

She shrugged again but this time pushed the pad across the bed to Carolyn. The words were carefully printed on the lined sheet of paper, as if they were meant to be read:

"My mother is the miasmic substance of which I breathe. A ubiquitous atmosphere I cannot live without.

"Allyson is a never-fading star. A celestial body whose brilliance hangs above me. Her brightness remains for me to be compared with; a brightness I can never achieve.

"James is an arrow. A sharp, narrow spear penetrating those areas I am too dull to touch. A shaft of perfection, broken in mid-flight.

"The soil on which I stand is Father. A loose matter which sinks beneath me and covers me each time I begin to grow.

"Michael is a stream. A cool, running body of water which will surge forward whether or not I stand in its path."

"I'm glad you've let me see this, Talia. Thank you very much," Carolyn wrote and returned the pad.

The next day Carolyn was hopeful as she and Talia continued to pass their notes back and forth. "Would you like to try liquid protein today?" Carolyn wrote, expecting Talia's written reply. "It would make it less difficult. You could do without the tubes."

"I want it to *be* difficult!" Talia screamed.

"*Why* do you want it difficult?" Carolyn asked aloud.

"You go away. You just leave me alone!"

When Carolyn returned that same afternoon, Talia met her at the door of her room with a fist full of papers. "I'm furious!" she said, urging Carolyn inside.

"Okay, let's talk about it."

"Do you know what they've done to me?" and Talia proceeded with a list of thirty-two accusations against her mother. "Look at this one," she said, grabbing Carolyn's arm, pointing to a sheet of paper on which she had scribbled each charge. "She insisted on dressing me in blue. All through adolescence she decided every day what I had to wear. She never *asked* if I cared. And this!" she pointed to another. "She's made all this fuss about me not eating, but it was she who always told me to leave off breads and chocolates. 'You're going to look exactly like your Aunt Helen,' she'd say. I wasn't Aunt Helen. I was a little girl. And *he* was just as bad."

"Who was just as bad? I can't know whom you're referring to unless you say people's names."

"Father, damn it! Father! 'I prefer my women thin,' he used to say. Well, *I* gave him thin and then what did he do? Nothing. Nothing but chastise me again."

The indictments ran for hours. Allyson had been a "crybaby" who had always gotten her way. Michael was "evolving into a parody of Father. He is trying to *bury* me," Talia said.

"How do you mean 'bury,' Talia?" Carolyn asked.

"Don't you even know what a metaphor is? You're as stupid as everyone else in this insipid place. You're a disgrace to your profession. Mother was correct for once, you *are* an empiric. An empiric, a charlatan, and a quack!"

Carolyn ignored the verbal lashing and encouraged Talia to continue with her list of complaints. After two days Talia seemed to tire physically from her rage, saying only, "They've done this to me. It's all their fault."

"All right, Talia, so it *is* their fault," Carolyn said, trying to turn the therapy around. "But maybe we should start concentrating on what you can do to correct things rather than continuing to blame."

"They smothered me!"

"Do you think blaming them is going to help?"

"You think I've done this to punish them, don't you? Well, look at *me*." She lifted the arm attached to the IV tube.

"I've told you we can take away the machine."

"I can't drink that other stuff."

"Why not?"

"I can't."

"Do you think you can try?"

On the following day she did try. "But I'm scared," she said, her hand trembling as she held the glass away from her as if the liquid smelled. "I don't feel guilty when I'm on the machine."

"You shouldn't feel guilty now."

She took a sip, spilled it down her chin, and started to cry. "It's going to make me fat."

"Talia, that's not going to happen. You're going to have to trust me."

Talia held a sketch pad at a distance, studied the paper, then turned it so Carolyn could see. She had drawn a simple caricature of one of the nurses. "You're talented, Talia," Carolyn said, examining the sketch. "This is extremely good."

"I could do one of you," she said, when Carolyn passed back the picture.

"I'd like that. And maybe you could draw one of yourself."

Talia turned from Carolyn to the paper and drew a circle. "This is the way I used to see myself. Empty and round. Empty of anything."

"How do you see yourself now?"

Talia was silent for a moment, then stood and moved from the bed. The fever she had developed when she first began to eat two and a half weeks ago had dropped, and she had now gained almost ten pounds. Her face showed she was getting rest, and there was a slight amount of color to her cheeks. "Do you think I look better?" she said, as she stood before a mirror.

"Absolutely. Do you?"

She touched her cheek and said: "I always wanted them to think I was pretty."

"Maybe your parents just didn't say it."

"But they should have," she said, angry again.

When she had gained fifteen pounds she decided to select her meals from the cafeteria menu herself. "I want it to be good food," she said, looking at a list of selections from the hospital dietician. "Good, natural, healthy food. Lean meats. Fruits and vegetables."

"Then that's what you'll have," Carolyn said.

A few days later Talia allowed Carolyn to be present as she ate. "I've been wondering," she said, as she carefully sliced her small portion of baked chicken, "if I might be able to see Michael now."

"Of course you can, if you want. How do you feel about that?"

"I don't know. I'm not sure. But we've been talking on the phone, and I think I want to see him. He's really not like Father, and . . ."

"Go on," Carolyn encouraged.

"No, I don't know what I was going to say. I don't remember."

"That's all right. Take your time. You're doing very well. I understand you weighed eighty-eight pounds today."

She suddenly panicked: "I think that's too much."

"Talia, why do you say that?"

"It's too much. I want to go back to the machine."

"You said you feel better this way. Stronger, more comfortable. More at ease."

"But I might hate myself. I might be losing control. I've been eating too much. I have to cut back!"

Over the next two days Talia cut her food intake in half. Then Carolyn asked, "Talia, what do you think are the most important characteristics a person can have?"

"Strength of character," Talia answered immediately. "Utilization of talent."

"Were you utilizing your talents before? Did you allow yourself time to draw? To write?"

"But I was strong."

"Were you?"

"You have to be strong not to eat," Talia defended.

"And you have to be strong to face your problems," Carolyn said.

Talia turned away and refused to answer, but she ordered a well-balanced lunch the next day.

"I thought I'd get here in time," Carolyn said when she walked into the hospital room. A small overnight case was packed and waiting at the foot of the bed.

"Michael will be here soon. I wanted to be ready." Talia stood near the windows, her arms close to her sides and her hands held behind her back.

"You look great."

Talia quickly looked down at her dress and then placed her hands in front of her. "I wish I felt that way."

"I thought you were excited," said Carolyn.

"Right now I guess I'm nervous."

"Most people are when they make a new move."

"But I'm only going home. Why should I be so scared?"

"Let's think about it for a minute. Why *are* you scared?"

"I don't know." She placed a hand on each arm. "I guess I'm afraid things will be different; or that they won't be different and I won't be able to cope."

"Different with Michael or with yourself?"

"I don't know—both. Mostly myself. I'm just not sure I have it all worked out."

"No one expects you to. We'll still be seeing each other several times a week," Carolyn said.

"What if I can't handle it? What if I stop eating again?"

"Do you think that's what you're going to do?"

"I don't know," Talia said. "That's what scares me."

20

A swatch of cloth lay on the car seat next to Carolyn. She studied it carefully while stopping for a light; ran her fingers across the raveled selvage and turned the triangle of chintz repeatedly in her hand. This simple piece of fabric, given to Carolyn weeks before, stood as a material representation of Talia's discovery of self. Her first thread of independence, pulled from glazed cotton.

Talia had discovered the fabric herself; found it and appreciated it because of her own unique taste, not because of someone else's suggestion. And in that fabric, Talia gained an expression of herself.

The total tapestry, the finished, complicated design which Carolyn now felt Talia was, had been difficult and slow to weave, the weft seemingly impossible at times in crossing the warp; the colors of her personality slow and belligerent in bringing together; the threads of her existence stubborn and laborious in the process of interlocking. It had taken months; tiresome months in which Carolyn herself wanted to abandon their therapeutic loom, leaving the threads separate, dangling, and undone. But each time she felt the need to leave, the growing textile gained a luminousness—a fascinating, resplendent quality all its own, the threads joining one another in vivid relief—and Carolyn, so inspired, would stay.

Carolyn folded the sample piece of material and slid it into her purse as she turned onto Anjaco Drive. Cars already lined the street in front of the pale yellow house. She parked, then hesitated a moment before leaving the car. There was an overshadowing anxiety mixed with the delight she felt for this particular evening. A fear she assumed only parents must know.

The party Mike and Talia gave tonight had been planned for nearly a month, since the day Carolyn told Talia she need only see her once every two weeks, and after three months, if things were going as well as she expected, then not at all. It was a party Talia and Mike had planned together, Carolyn knew, as husband and wife. A step they had taken together for Mike's career. Yet, in spite of the obvious reasons for the party, Carolyn knew there was more. It was an undeclared "coming out"; a debut for Talia; her first public encounter with reality. And it was this, Carolyn realized, which frightened her; an ominous dread much as a mother might feel watching the emergence of a child coming of age; pleased, yet filled with apprehension that the child might fail.

Carolyn was met at the front door of the home by Talia, even before ringing the bell.

"I'm so glad," Talia said, reaching out for Carolyn's hand, pulling her inside. "I was afraid you might not be able to come. You might be too busy."

"Are you kidding? I wouldn't have missed this for the world." Carolyn tried to intonate lightness, trying not to display too much attachment, too much emotion or fear.

"I thought you would try," Talia said. "I mean, I hoped you would." She dropped Carolyn's hand and took her purse and wrap. In that moment in which they had touched, Talia's hand was warm and soft; far from the skeletal appendage Carolyn had held months ago when Talia lay in a hospital bed.

From the light of candles which flickered on a foyer table, Carolyn admired the dignity and classically carved features of Talia's face. The sharp profile, Carolyn knew, had been inherited from Talia's mother; the same strong, prominent lines. But, with her new fullness, Talia now possessed a quiet serenity unknown to Mrs. Sinclaire. And her smile showed confidence, maturity; while release from her illness had taken years off her face.

Carolyn scanned the length of Talia's body, visually showing approval. "Talia, you look terrific," she said.

"You think so? That's what Michael said." Talia stood back, touching the sides of her dress. "You like it? I chose it myself." She turned full circle now so Carolyn might see. The soft coral, far from the mournful colors Talia had worn while ill, hugged the newformed, well-rounded body and showed off the femininity of her hips and breasts. "It was a surprise, for Michael," she said.

"I love it," said Carolyn.

"You don't think it's too much?"

"I think it's perfect."

She took Carolyn's hand again. "There are so many people you'll want to meet," she said. "I think every airline in the country is represented here tonight. The living room's full." She led Carolyn from the foyer.

The back of Talia's head was a smooth veil of dark, recently trimmed hair. She turned around before they entered the filled room and spoke in a conspiratorial whisper: "Everything's going quite well."

"Did you doubt that it would?"

"A little; yes." She started to go, then added: "I'm glad you're here."

In the living room Talia introduced Carolyn to a couple standing near the entrance: "Dr. Stepler," she said, now holding Carolyn at the arm, "I want you to meet the Grahams. They flew in from San Francisco this afternoon." All timidity was gone now from Talia's voice. She faced the couple, positive, self-assured. "Dr. Stepler attended school there. University of California. Elizabeth, keep her company for a moment, won't you? I want to get Michael."

"No, Talia, please; don't bother," Carolyn said.

"Don't be silly. He'll want to *see* you."

Carolyn nodded automatically as the Grahams spoke, answered their questions by rote and watched Talia as she wound her way through the room. "I love your outfit," she said to an older woman she passed, taking the woman's hand. And to another: "We were so excited you were able to come." Carolyn followed the strong, clear voice, and the well-carried body until it was hidden among guests, taking pride, still as a parent might, for having been part of its redevelopment.

When Carolyn no longer saw a trace of the reddish dress, she looked about the large, high-ceilinged room. She had been curious about Talia's taste, had wondered what she had done with her home after declaring she was going to "redo" and rid her house of Mother. And now as Carolyn looked about her, the room *was* Talia; a culmination of all Carolyn knew Talia had once been and all she had now become. The same chintz Carolyn held in her purse now covered the sofa and chairs; the clean white walls were accentuated with delicate paintings and prints. Classics lined the shelves and Chinese porcelain was displayed on the mantel and low rosewood tables. The effect was refined, sophisticated, and subtle. And Carolyn felt suddenly and pleasantly comforted, protected even, by Talia's home.

They returned, husband and wife, Talia leading Mike by the arm. "Oh, did you meet Mrs. Winston?" she asked Mike and stopped to introduce him to the woman. "She has a son at United too." As Mike greeted his guest, Talia let go, and as she stood alone, Carolyn saw, she stood as confidently as one as she had as two.

Talia took his arm again as they approached Carolyn. Mike extended a hand and Talia brushed against Carolyn's side. And for that brief instant, they all touched, an ephemeral bond of affection running through the three. But Mike pulled away, avoiding Carolyn's eyes, almost as quickly and as instinctively as he had reached out.

"She looks great, doesn't she?" He put his arm around Talia's waist.

"Terrific. I told her so."

"Guess what she weighs?"

Talia held up an arm and turned it comically for Carolyn's estimation.

"One fifteen," Carolyn said.

"You're high and Michael was low." Talia said it with a child's sense of glee, as if she had outsmarted them in a game which had once been the most critical aspect of her life. "One twelve. Excellent, I'd say."

"So would I," said Carolyn.

Mike shifted, then offered Carolyn a drink.

"Yes, please, I'd like that," she said.

Talia stopped him as he started to leave. "Let me," she said. "You introduce Dr. Stepler around and I'll take care of the drinks."

"Talia, I'll do it."

"No, Michael, please. I want to."

She moved away, stopping to speak to the Grahams, who now stood by themselves. "May I get you anything?" she said. "Of course, you can help me," and she and Mrs. Graham walked through the room together. "Do you know Elizabeth?" Carolyn could hear her say, introducing the woman to someone else. "Her husband's with Northwest Orient," and: "Oh, good, you've met."

"She's handling it well, isn't she?" Mike said. Carolyn nodded, angered for feeling the slightest twinge at the way he looked at Talia. "Let's get out of the crowd," he said.

She followed him, waiting behind as he paused to chat, not wanting to be introduced. "Hello, Bill." He touched a man's arm. "I didn't see you come in." They shook hands.

"Expecting Stoner to show?" the man said.

"He said he'd be here. May I get you a drink?"

"The logistics are right," someone else said. "Free booze and beautiful women. He'll be here."

Mike laughed. He seemed outwardly confident, but there was a nervous tide, Carolyn sensed, flowing below the façade.

He halted when they reached the far side of the room. "Sit down?" he said.

"No, thanks. I'm fine."

"She does look good, doesn't she?" He still avoided Carolyn's eyes.

"Yes, Mike, she does."

"I mean healthy and all. She looks healthy, doesn't she?"

"She is healthy."

"I still can't believe it." He gazed at a point across the room. "I mean, I wake up some mornings expecting things to be the same, expecting to find her downstairs on that damn bicycle. But instead she's beside me. Asleep. And I'm scared I might have dreamt it. I'm afraid of that right now; afraid I've been dreaming."

"You haven't been."

"Look at her tonight and then remember the way she was a few months ago. It seems impossible. The change. I believed for so long she's never be well that it seems unreal now that she is." Now he met her eyes. "Has she recovered, Carolyn? I mean completely. No possibility of relapse?"

"An anorexic is cured only when the bizarre things she formerly did are totally repulsive to her. From observing Talia, listening to her, being as rational as I think I'm capable of being, yes, I think she's cured."

"Carolyn—I can never thank you—"

"Don't worry," she teased to forestall sentiment, "I'll think of a way." At the moment she said it, a ghost of their former relationship appeared between them, an apparition which sobered them both in its flirtation with the past. She looked about the room, voice lifting. "Why don't I know anyone? I thought all the old Coastal people would be here?"

"There are no old Coastal people. I'm one of the few who survived the merger. Stoner's revamped the entire operation."

"Is that good?"

"Not for those who got tossed out on their ear."

"No, I mean for the company. Is what Frank's doing beneficial on the whole?"

"His supporters think so." His response was practiced, politic. "They seem to regard him as a legal and financial wizard."

"Is he?"

"Frank Stoner's the same fool he's always been. I try to stay out of his way."

"You're backing down?"

"Trying to play it safe, Carolyn. Survive."

"And that's what the party is all about."

"This evening may be my salvation. Building bridges, Carolyn. If Stoner's shrewd, I have to be shrewder. Make every contact I can. I have to—" He stopped, smiling as Talia walked toward them with drinks and hors d'oeuvres.

"Scotch for you," Talia said, giving a glass to Mike. "And wine for the doctor and myself."

"Talia, the name is Carolyn. I wish you'd call me that."

She stared at Carolyn a moment, then handed her the wine. "No, not yet." She turned to Mike. "I spoke with the man from Eastern, Michael. Jennings, isn't it?"

"Yes. What'd he say?"

"That he wanted to see you. And I'm not sure, but I think I was being flirted with."

"Is that right?" Mike said, and they laughed.

"Jealous." She smiled at Carolyn. "Try the food, Dr. Stepler, you'll love it. I didn't cook one thing for this party myself, did I, Michael?"

"Not a thing."

"We ordered everything from Cloudt's. I was too busy with the party; new clothes. The guest list was over a hundred people."

Mike shifted at Carolyn's side. "I think I'll leave you two alone for a while," he said. "I need to mingle with our guests."

"Be sure and speak to Mr. Jennings, Michael. His wife's name is Helen," Talia said.

"Yes, I will. Can I bring you anything?"

Talia returned his smile. "No, I'm fine."

"There he is!" A voice boomed from behind, and Carolyn saw Talia stiffen. "Michael the host, I need a drink!" Carolyn turned to see Frank Stoner striding toward them, holding an empty glass.

"Well! Isn't this a surprise?" Stoner said as he saw Carolyn and slid an arm around her neck. "What's the good doctor doing here? I thought you resigned."

"I did."

"I *see*." He winked at Mike. "Ah, romance!"

"Come on, Frank," Mike forced a laugh. "Let's get that drink."

"What's the hurry? I haven't seen this beautiful broad in months." He spoke to Carolyn: "Listen, why don't you drop this four-eyed flunky kid and let me show you a good time."

It was as if Carolyn were watching some horrendous accident take place before her eyes; she couldn't speak or move. Mike, his face drawn, also seemed mute and unable to take action.

"Now that you don't have your love junkets to Miami and Chicago, he won't be any fun anymore." Stoner's voice had subdued conversation around them. He turned to Mike: "Sorry about that, old boy. Curtailed expenses make happy stockholders. And older men make better lovers," he said to Carolyn.

Talia stared at Carolyn and took a backward step.

"Talia," Mike reached out. "Talia, listen—"

Frank snapped with awareness. "Talia? I—I didn't know. I didn't recognize you." He turned to Carolyn: "I didn't see her." And then to Mike: "Man, I didn't know."

Carolyn lifted a hand to touch Talia and as she did, Talia recoiled, then turned and moved through the hushed room.

=21=

"She's been gone for two days, Carolyn."

"I realize that."

"What's happening to her?"

"I've told you, I don't know." Carolyn stepped from the elevator at the eighth floor.

Mike seized her arm. "You're the psychiatrist. Why don't you know?" A janitor turned and stared.

"Lower your voice." She removed his hand. "Let's go to my office where we can talk."

"She took the Audi; the tires were bad. There might have been a wreck."

"I've called the police. Hospitals. There's been no accident."

Carolyn fumbled for her keys. Impatiently Mike took them and opened the office door.

"She doesn't know how to change a flat tire," he said when they were inside. "I was going to teach her, when there was time."

Carolyn dropped her briefcase into a chair and walked to the desk.

"I need a drink," he said. "Do you have anything to drink."

"I don't keep anything alcoholic here."

"She didn't say a word. She just walked out the door and got in the car. Not a word. Carolyn, what's going through her head?"

"Mistrust, probably. A feeling of being abandoned."

"Where the hell would she go for two days?"

"My first guess would be home; to her parents."

"I called there; they haven't seen her. It was a stupid move to call," he said. "Stupid."

"Sit down, Mike. I'll make coffee."

"I thought maybe they had lied. I drove to Athens and sat outside the house for hours, waiting."

"And Talia didn't show?"

"I shouldn't have called them."

"How did they react?"

"Angry. Accusing. I had to tell them why. About us, I mean."

Carolyn spilled coffee grounds. "Then they know I'm involved? They're aware of our affair?"

"If it's your reputation you're worried about—"

"You know that's not my concern."

"What is your concern, goddamn it? Don't give me all that crap about 'my poor patient.' You don't give a damn about Talia and never have."

Carolyn met his eyes levelly; her response was even: "If you truly believed that, you would have removed her from my care. Sit down. The coffee'll be ready in a moment."

She turned to the percolator, very much aware of his being right behind her.

"Why would you take Talia as a patient?"

Carolyn moved sideways. "I need an aspirin," she said. "Want one?"

"I'd like an answer."

She placed two white tablets on her tongue and followed them with water.

"Why her? You said you were quitting Coastal because your practice demanded more time. You didn't need another patient. So why did you take her?"

Carolyn kept her voice calm. "Because you asked me."

"Bullshit!"

"Begged me, as I recall."

"Had you not wanted to take her I could have begged forever and it wouldn't have done any good. I was the last person in the world who should have made that judgment. My wife was dying before my eyes, and that idiot doctor was only making matters worse. I was scared to death and you knew it."

"I took her because she was your wife and needed help."

"The very reason you shouldn't have taken her. Because she *was* my wife."

"If you think blaming me for this somehow exonerates you, you're wrong. You were fully aware of the possible consequences. If you want to blame someone, blame the Sinclaires. Or blame yourself, and I'll accept my share along with you."

He reached for a chair and sat down. "I lost my job."

"I'm sorry, Mike. Truly."

"When I went to the office yesterday, Stoner had changed all the locks. All my things were out in the hall. The bastard." He massaged his unshaven face with both hands. "Actually, it was the smartest thing he could have done. I wasn't his friend before, and if he didn't know it then, he knows we're enemies now. I would have sabotaged the goddamn company, if necessary, to sink the son-of-a-bitch."

Carolyn stayed trembling fingers as she poured coffee, but the cup jiggled as she served Mike. He took the cup, grabbed her hand, and looked up with reddened eyes.

"I'm sorry, Carolyn," he said.

"There's no reason to be."

He was hunched forward, the cup gripped between his hands. "I haven't slept for two days. Thinking about everything. You know, it's ironic; some of the things that drew me to Talia were actually indications of her illness. The way she applied herself to her studies. Always so serious about them. Her perfectionism. I really admired that. I admired her intellect. I even admired that pompous ass father of hers. My parents were uneducated. Did I tell you that?"

"Yes, Mike."

"When I first met Sinclaire, he awed me with all those philosophical thoughts and high-minded quotes.

It took me years to realize he had no philosophy of his own, that all those quotes camouflaged the things he thought he lacked. Talia worked so hard to please him so I thought if I was like him in some ways, she'd work as hard to please me. I perpetuated the problem. I thought she needed a father figure, and I tried to be one. The truth is—I didn't need a little girl, and she didn't need a father. And that's what we both had."

Carolyn resisted the impulse to go to him. Sitting at her desk she used the proven technique of saying nothing to mask her own feelings.

"She isn't going to come back, is she?" he said.

"I think she will."

"She won't come back."

"She'll come home, Mike. I'm certain she will."

"I never wanted anything the way I wanted Talia. I had never known anyone like her. I loved her gentleness, her understanding, her eagerness to please. I struggled to succeed not so much for myself, but to be worthy in the eyes of her parents."

"In the beginning I thought her illness was a punishment for me; because I wasn't adequate. The things I was trying to be for her, were the things she was trying to fight. I only increased the problem." He looked up at Carolyn.

"You had no way of knowing she was ill," Carolyn said.

"But you did. You should never have accepted her as a patient. With your training you should have known what would happen if she found out about us."

"Mike, I warned you months ago that she knew you were having an affair."

"You said she suspected."

"The first step to sure knowledge," Carolyn said.

"Then you should have dropped her. Sent her to someone else."

"She was beginning to make progress. And I felt it would be wrong to make a change in therapists again."

"It just occurred to me—you knew I was going to lose my job months ago, didn't you? For months you had Talia coming in here, three times a week, consuming a third of my income. And nothing happens. Then suddenly, with the company merger making my days at Coastal numbered, you decided to put Talia into the hospital at last. And miraculously she gained weight, got rosy cheeks, and she's healthy."

"That's so childish I won't even respond."

"Carolyn, what is she going to do? Will she hurt herself?"

"You mean physically?"

"Suicide. Will she kill herself?"

Carolyn clasped cold hands. "She's stronger now. She knows herself better."

"But what does that mean? Is she going to come home?"

"Mike, what the hell do you expect of me?"

"You're the psychiatrist. You've spent all these months with her. You've listened to every intimate detail of her life. You should know what thoughts go through her head."

"I'm a psychiatrist, not a psychic. I can't know what she's thinking."

"Then, damn it, give me your considered opinion. Give me a guess."

"Mike, most people who've been ill and gone through therapy are actually stronger than those of us so-called well-balanced and untested personalities. I say again, she's stronger now. Perhaps stronger than either of us."

"If I were in her place I'd be blind with anger. I'd be plotting murder of you, me, both of us."

"But you wouldn't do it, and neither will Talia." There was a pause, and then she said: "Mike, this is getting us nowhere. Go home and get some rest."

He looked at her, his head shaking slightly. "I still want to know why you took her as a patient. A form of female retaliation? Jealous reasoning?"

"Oh, please, don't be stupid. I don't know why."

"The hell you don't. You've had a motive behind every move made in your life."

He stood beside her and waited.

"Well, all right, if you insist on psychoanalyzing me, I did it because I had an interest in anorexia. My mother once lost a patient, an anorexic. I think it must have been the only disappointment in her illustrious career. The parents insisted on removing the child from therapy because they were unsatisfied with the rate of progress. The girl died from a perforated ulcer two weeks later."

"Because of your mother?"

"That was years ago. It aroused my interest in the subject. As it turns out, we can both be thankful for it. Otherwise I might not have recognized the symptoms for what they were and they might have been treated improperly."

"Because of your mother! Then you really didn't care about Talia."

"Perhaps I cared more than I should have. Talia told me one time that I was afraid of getting too close. She was right. I am. I was afraid of getting too close to you, even. I was relieved when our relationship ended. It has always frightened me when I begin to care."

Mike looked not at her, but through and beyond. "Will she revert to the way she was? To starving again?"

"I can't be sure."

After a moment he moved to the door. He spoke with his back to her: "Whatever your motives, you should not have accepted Talia as a patient. We may have killed her, you and I."

It was dark now, both inside Carolyn's office and out, and she had been alone for hours. She looked about her; this had always been enough to comfort her, these four walls, the books which lined them, the grass cloth, the tweed, the Carrara marble. But it all seemed hollow now, a room full of objects. *It has always frightened me when I begin to care.* It was frightening now to admit that; to realize she had no one to comfort her but herself. There was no one to turn to; no one to cry with; no one to condone or condemn her mistakes, to listen to her fears. And the worst fear she had ever experienced was knowing now she was completely alone.

She lowered her head to the desk, rubbed her eyes, then stared at the phone. The telephone number came suddenly, clearly, as if she had dialed it yesterday rather than months ago. She touched the receiver, then slowly removed it and dialed. The long-distance line sounded with static, then signaled a ring. The sound of the voice which answered was strong and familiarly reassuring, giving her confidence she had done the right thing. "It's Carolyn," she spoke softly. "I've made a terrible mistake, and I'm afraid." She paused, then said what she had always wanted to say: "Mother, I need your help."

22

Blood spotted the bed. It was warm and wet under Talia, drawing her from sleep. Turning on a light, she examined, touched it: vermilion over white. A blood-blot Rorschach waiting for interpretation.

"It's a glorious red, girls! A beautiful red," the seventh-grade gym teacher had said. Talia had never looked.

"You're menstruating, Talia Victoria," Mother had said. "You're capable of having babies now." Babies came to adults; those able to handle responsibility.

"Every female in the world menstruates," the health-and-hygiene film had explained. "Every female in the world." Every female minus one.

Talia touched the stain again. It was darkening, not ominously, but naturally; a flat, Gauguin red. There were no serpents hidden within its redness, no bleeding evils. It was warm, wet, miraculously clean. The blot was round; a tidy circle expanding slowly, unto itself. Unique and complete.

Bathed and dressed now, Talia stood outside the motel-room door, beside the Audi. She pulled a sweater about her for warmth against the morning. Thirty miles to the east, to her left, lay Athens. Atlanta was the same direction to the right. She drove west. Leaving a mark of herself behind.

Headlights from the Audi illuminated Michael's Porsche as Talia pulled into the drive. The Porsche, instead of being safely housed in the garage as always, had been parked outside, abandoned; the door on the driver's side had been left agape, allowing morning to enter and sit upon the leather.

The house, as if Talia had returned to it after being a child, appeared smaller, closer to the ground. And the trees which surrounded it were no longer a fortress, but wispy, waving verticals such as Mondrian had drawn.

The Audi coughed and choked to a temporary death as Talia removed the key. She walked, under the shroud of early hours which the sun had not yet tried to penetrate, to the Porsche and closed and locked its door. And as she walked the bricked sidewalk and climbed the front steps, her movements and surroundings were familiar to her; not as if remembering them from four days ago, but from another life.

Inside, she walked among overloaded ashtrays and half-empty glasses, an interloper prowling among the scattered remnants of someone else's party. Litter stared at her, the intruder, as she made each turn; mold overtaking the remains of food, smells of gin and vermouth arising from fingerprinted vessels. She picked up a glass, then another, then suddenly, as if being burned, put them both back down.

She crossed through the dining room, trays of food and unstoppered bottles of liquor piled on the table. The air was full of onion and garlic and the stench of spoiling shellfish. She pushed against the door to the kitchen, a hand held over mouth and nose, the portal swinging open with a squeak she seemed faintly to remember.

As she moved through the doorway, her hand went to the wall, feeling for a switch. She found it; pushed up; the room filled with light.

Michael put a hand over his face, shielding his eyes from the sudden light. He sat slumped in a straight-backed chair, pulled close to the kitchen table. He rubbed his eyes, then looked up at her, still shielding them with a hand cupped at his forehead. He was unshaven, his hair oily and plastered to his scalp. His clothes were filthy, the same ones he had worn at the party.

"Are you all right?" he said, voice gravelly, as if he had been asleep.

"Are *you?*" she said, and he scraped his chair across the floor to stand just as she was seated.

"You all right?" he said again.

"Yes, Michael, fine."

He ran a hand roughly up and down his face, across his head, the hair sticking out where he had rubbed. She studied him, trying to familiarize herself with this man which another mind and body had known and married. He seemed paler, thinner.

"You want something?" he said. "Coffee?"

She shook her head. There was a bottle of Scotch, open and near-empty, on the table. Beside the liquor was a vial of small white pills. Talia looked from the vial to Michael and then back again to the pills. He followed her eyes.

"I didn't," he said distantly. "I was a coward. Been contemplating it all night. All boils down to being a coward. Afraid to die." He looked up from the vial he now held and stared at her. "You bought new clothes," he said. "I worried."

"I had credit cards." She controlled her voice.

"They look nice." She watched his Adam's apple leap up and down. "I'll make you coffee," he said, starting to stand.

"No, Michael. I don't care for anything. I only came for a few of my things. Some clothes."

He sat back down. "You're leaving," It was a statement.

"For a while, yes."

He leaned forward, and for a moment she thought he was going to touch her. "I thought the worst that could happen would be for you to be dead. But the worst—" she watched the apple jump again, and her throat was dry as she too swallowed. "The worst is just to lose you."

"I'm not sure you ever had me to lose."

"You never loved me?"

"It's not that. You see, the person you lived with, even the person you married, that was someone else, Michael. I don't even know that girl."

"You came back to leave me."

"Michael, she was a different person. *I* need to learn who you and I are."

"I knew you would." He held his head between his hands. "Knew you'd leave me."

"Michael . . ."

"Talia, don't go. Not now, please. Talia, I've—" he took her hand. "I've been crazy; afraid you were dead. Afraid if you weren't, you might not come back. Talia, if you go, I've lost all that is important to me. Please don't leave me now."

"Michael, I need some time."

"I could give you time."

"I mean alone. Michael, someone else married you. I'm not that girl. I need time to make decisions. To know if you're really the person I should be with the rest of my life."

"Talia, I didn't mean for it to happen. Any of it. I never wanted you to know."

"I don't condemn you for that, not now. I can't. What you did, you did not to me, but to someone else. You did it to Talia Sinclaire, a very ill and frightened woman. I also know why you did it. I've had hours to think it over. You needed something which the other girl, the other Talia, wasn't able to give. I realize that now."

"It happened, Talia. I swear, I didn't seek it out. It just happened."

"Do you love her, Michael?"

"No."

"The thing I need from you now is honesty. I think I can withstand anything, so long as it's the truth."

"You have to believe it, Talia. I swear to you, I don't love her."

"Do you know what's ironic about that?" she said. He was holding her hands; he looked tired and sad.

"It's that I *do* love her. Or at least I don't feel any hate. I'm not positive it's not some kind of patient-doctor thing I still feel. Maybe it is. But if I tried to stack my emotions one atop the other, the person at the point of the pyramid would be Dr. Stepler. Maybe right now she's the only person who truly knows me, or rather the only person *I* truly know."

He withdrew his hands.

"Michael, I don't mean to hurt you with what I said."

"Where've you been?"

"Home first. Athens."

"Carolyn said you would."

"I drove right up to the house. I even stopped the car. But I didn't go in. It wasn't my house." She watched to see his reaction. He looked at her quickly, then turned away. "After that I drove to Brunswick. We used to go there when I was a child. I suppose I thought I'd find something there. Perhaps I did. I learned I didn't want to die either, Michael."

She studied his face. It showed no emotion.

"I stayed an entire day on Jekyll Island, walking the beach, wanting to die. I thought of gathering stones the way Virginia Woolf did, placing them in my pockets to weight me so I would drown. Do you know why I didn't, Michael?" His back was to her now. "I didn't deserve to die. Dr. Stepler taught me that. She taught me that I deserve to live."

He turned and faced her.

"And the other reason, Michael, was because it seemed cowardice *to* do it. And for once in my life, I wanted to be brave. Do you see that? The difference? All those horrible months I starved myself, going through unbelievable pain, I thought I was proving something; proving how brave I was. But don't you see it, Michael? I wasn't being brave at all. I was hiding behind my illness because I was frightened by life.

"When I left Jekyll, I just drove. I don't even remember where. Just drove until I needed gas. I finally ended up between here and Athens. I went to a little place outside of Stone Mountain and purchased clothes and shampoo. I ate dinner in a restaurant. By myself, Michael. I ordered and paid for it myself. Then I drove to a motel. I'd never done that before— checked into a place by myself. Paid for things myself. I bought a toothbrush, and Michael, for the first time in my life, I decided what color my damn toothbrush would be. For the first time I was totally independent. I didn't need anyone but me, and what I decided was okay. Michael, can you understand what that means? To decide what kind of toothpaste you're going to buy? To check into a motel and sign your own name?"

"You're going to divorce me, aren't you?"

"Michael, I need to learn if I love you as the other Talia did. I'm not sure I really know you, don't you understand?"

"You're so forgiving of Carolyn."

"The only one I begrudge at the present is myself. I robbed myself of a great deal. I'm trying to understand why."

"She's as much to blame as I am, Talia."

"I'm not sure anyone's to blame. That's what I'm trying to tell you. Not even Mother and Father, possibly. I demanded things of myself." She took his hand. "I need some time, Michael."

"What do you plan to do?"

"I'd like to have an apartment of my own. Just for a while. A small one, so I can be by myself. I'll need to borrow the money from you at first, until I get acclimated; get going on my own."

"I can't."

"It shouldn't cost a great deal."

"I can't give it to you, Talia."

"I plan to get a job. I'll repay you."

"Do you know the worst part of failure?" He was crying. "It's knowing it's all probably your own fault. You truly can't blame it on anyone but yourself."

"Michael—"

"I can't give you the money, Talia."

"I could—"

"I've lost my job." He dropped back into the chair. "I've been fired."

"I didn't know."

"I've lost everything."

She knelt beside him.

"I spent our money like a fool. We've been living far beyond our means since we married. I have your doctor bills to pay. Hospital expenses."

"You can find another job."

"Where? I've been fired. There's a stigma to that."

"We could speak with someone. Mr. Stoner. Have it removed from your record."

"I wouldn't do that."

"Why? Because of pride?"

"I have no more pride."

"You should. I'm proud of you." He turned to her. "You stayed with me when I was ill. I gave you bad times, I know that now. Not many men would have stuck it out as you did. You were loyal."

"How can you say that? I cheated on you, Talia."

"You needed something I couldn't give. If you were hungry you would go for food, wouldn't you?"

"We may lose the house."

"Michael, we don't need the house."

"Your parents already hate me. They know why you left. When they find out about the job . . ."

"My parents aren't the ones who matter now. They have their own lives. We should have ours." She stroked his head, pushing away hair from around his face. He seemed older, yet at the same time a child.

"I always thought the worst possible failure would be this—losing my job. The humiliation. The embarrassment. But it doesn't compare to the failure I feel for losing you."

"Michael—"

"Talia, I know what I've done to you. I detest myself for some of the things. Cruel things. I wasn't understanding."

"I don't blame you for that."

"But I blame myself. I've had three days to think

about it. To wallow in and out of self-pity. To blame Carolyn, your parents, Stoner, even you for the things I did to you, for losing my job. But when it comes right down to it, there's no one to blame but myself. Talia, I'm guilty on many counts and I know it, but I'm begging you to stay." The tears swelled again. "I'm not sure I would do it for you, but I'm asking you to do it for me."

"Michael, you went to Dr. Stepler because I wasn't able to give you what you needed. I'm still not sure I can. I don't think I've fully learned or come to grips with the sexual aspects of myself. Can you live with that?"

"I think so."

"I'm still frightened at times of what lies ahead. It frightens me, too, to think of the things I once did. It's terrifying to think I might ever do that again. Maybe I'm still not certain I'm totally well, you know? I have this need to rely on crutches, as a person might fear falling after being lame; afraid to put all their weight on the bad leg."

"All right, Talia."

"And I need to know you, to understand who and what you are. In a way, your wife has died, and you and I are married to strangers now. It's going to take a little more time."

"I can make it up to you, Talia," he said.

"We both need to make things up to ourselves."

"Just don't leave me again. Please."

"No. I won't leave."

23

A Matisse print hung on the reception room wall: *Large Decoration with Masks*. It was always the first object Talia saw upon entering the room. She had always thought the paper cut-outs trivial, probably because Mother loved Matisse so. But still, the piece represented a continuity. There was order in the work: yet a certain freedom, or spontaneity, surrounding the two like heads.

Talia turned from the print to the door, the one which opened to Dr. Stepler's office. She could still flee if she wanted. She could quietly slip from the room and run. No; she had come this far. She must not run.

She turned again to the huge print over the sofa. This time the heads were similar but not exactly alike. And the objects around each, although creating harmony, were also not the same. She moved to sit under the print. As she did so, the door opened, slowly, and she watched as Dr. Stepler emerged.

"Hello, Talia." The woman stood tall and erect, a beam of light in the doorway. Her hair fell upon her shoulders, matching the pale yellow of her dress. "Please, come in," she said.

Talia walked inside, and as they passed in the doorway, realized they were almost identical in size.

"Please, have a seat." And instead of sitting opposite one another, as they had always done, they sat side by side. "It's good to see you, Talia. It's been a while."

"Yes." Talia said it clearly. "Since the party."

The doctor quickly stood. "I'll have Freddie bring us coffee."

"No—thank you. I can't stay." Talia watched carefully as she sat back down and wondered if it was some kind of feminine jealousy which made her think this woman not as beautiful as she had thought before.

"I—" They spoke at the same time, then faltered, each waiting for the other.

"I'm sorry. Go ahead."

Talia hesitated, then said: "We're moving. I came to say good-bye."

"Are you moving far?"

"Dallas. Michael has a new job."

"Talia, I'm glad."

Talia studied the doctor's expression, finding only honesty there.

"I'll be working too," Talia said now. "In a small art gallery outside the city."

"Good. That sounds like something you'll enjoy."

"For a while anyway, until we're settled and I know more what I want to do." There was a pause, then Talia added: "He's been fine, if you're wondering."

"I'm wondering more about you. Are you fine, Talia?"

"I weigh nearly a hundred fifteen pounds, if that's what you mean. And the fact that I do doesn't scare me. I'm glad Michael thinks I look well. He does," she said hurriedly. "He's not just telling me, I'm sure."

"I'm sure, too. You look better than you ever have. You look wonderful, in fact."

Another pause, then Talia admitted: "I started to call you a couple of times."

"I wish you had."

"I always got scared; then angry. I've hated you at times."

There was a long silence in which they both shifted and recrossed their legs. The discomfort of the silence was lessened by the synchronization of their movements; Talia wondered if Matisse did not have a subtle hand in the act.

"I started to call you, too, Talia." It was said at last.

"Only I didn't know what to say. All I can say now is, I'm sorry."

"Michael needed something," Talia said, angry now. "I can understand why he did it. But why did *you?*"

"I needed the same things he did, Talia—affection, companionship, someone to talk with—only without getting involved."

"That's what confuses me. Michael says he loved me, and I believe that."

"Yes, you should."

"I do. And I also believe he didn't want to get involved. But that's what I don't understand. You had no one else; why didn't you?"

"I guess—" The doctor stalled and walked to the far side of the room. She ran her fingers along the back of the Bufano, then cupped her hand under its neck, as if to strangle the sculpture. "I guess I thought as long as I didn't get involved, I couldn't get hurt. Actually, you recognized that long before I did, Talia," she said, turning back around. "You always knew there are far worse things than being hurt."

She returned to her seat, then leaned toward her former patient. "How's your mother, Talia?"

"She's had a stroke."

"Is she all right?"

Talia said: "There's still paralysis of her right side, and it's difficult for her to talk. It's very sad. But somehow it's brought us closer together—the stroke and the anorexia—though in many ways we're further apart."

"How about your father?"

"He's well. I think Mother's needing him has made him—I'm not sure what the word is—stronger, I guess. But really more gentle, if you understand."

"Yes, it makes sense."

"I felt guilty about Mother at first. I thought it was my fault."

"Do you now?"

"I worry about them both, but I think that's only natural." She looked to the doctor for confirmation.

"Yes," she said, "it is."

Talia glanced at her watch. "I'd better go." She looked about the room; a hollow chamber; nothing to hold her. There had never been sadness for her in leaving things; only people. She started to stand, then looked at the woman evenly. "I trusted you," she said.

"Do you think I could have told you, Talia?"

"I guess I really don't know."

They both stood, equal, yet different, then walked in rhythm away from the chairs.

"Thank you for coming, Talia. For making the move."

They stopped when they reached the door. "About Michael," Talia said. "He *is* doing fine." The doctor nodded as if she understood. "I'm learning things about him I wasn't able to see when I was ill. He's a good person. And I think we're going to make it, now that we're not so preoccupied with ourselves. At least I hope so." Talia reached for the door. "Good-bye, Carolyn."

"You're going to be okay, Talia."

"Yes, I'm going to be fine," she said and walked through the office, past the Matisse, and out the door.

About the Author

Emily Ellison Hudlow was born in Dalton, Georgia, in 1951 and educated in Ft. Lauderdale, Florida, and at the University of Georgia. She now lives with her husband Tom in Fairhope, Alabama, where she wrote ALABASTER CHAMBERS, her first novel.